THE QUEEN

SKYE WARREN

PROLOGUE
DAMON

THE WINTER AIR seeps into the cracks of my bones, the seams of my skin. There are a million places where my body has broken and reformed. A million times that I remember with each gust of wind.

Despite the temperature I have my coat open, my hands on the rail. Showing weakness isn't an option. My heart would stop beating, my lungs would stop breathing before I shivered even once. Any hint of weakness was stamped out of me a long time ago.

The man who approaches me looks left and right. God, he's a sitting duck if anyone wanted to shoot him. The very picture of weakness. His cheeks are ruddy, eyes red. His puffy coat must provide decent warmth, but still he rubs his hands together in his cheap knit gloves.

He comes to stand beside me, looking out over the water. "Some weather," he says.

A sitting duck, but he's under my protection now.

On the other side of this river is a college teaming with bright-eyed kids. Brightly colored banners decorate the staid green lawn. This far away I can't read them, but I can guess what they say. *Welcome to Orientation. Join the math club. Sign up for this sorority.*

"Some weather," I say, because I'm as much of a sitting duck as he is.

At least when it comes to this girl.

"I saw the dorm room," the man offers. "Kind of small, but I guess that's the way of it. Got her moved in okay. She didn't have much stuff."

"You'll send her extra money," I say softly.

Knit gloves rub together. "Right. Of course. And I'll be doing some work for you, then?"

What kind of work do you give a man who fails at everything? What kind of work do you give the father of the girl you can't have? "Collections."

It's a dirty job. A violent one. "Yes," he says, bobbing his head. "Yes, I can do that."

Some boys have started a game of football. I can see them chasing after each other like fucking morons from here. What must it be like to run away for sport instead of necessity? What must it be like to tackle other men for fun instead of survival?

There are people on the perimeter of the makeshift game. Maybe some boys who want to watch the action. Some girls checking out the players. Is Penny among them? Does she see something she likes?

No, she wouldn't be there. She would have found some library by now. Some quiet place to read.

"When you gamble again…" I say, letting the thought hang in the air.

"I won't."

This is a lie. Of course he will. "When you gamble again, I'm not going to kill you."

"I understand," he says hastily, probably assuming I'm implying some kind of torture.

"I'm not going to kill you, because for reasons beyond my comprehension, that girl gives a shit what happens to you. So you had better keep it that way, old man."

He grasps the cold railing, leaning heavily on it. "I see. And what are your intentions with her?"

It feels strange to laugh in a real way. Not the kind of pretend amusement that I walk around with on a daily basis. This laugh shakes my whole body. "Are you really going to have the talk with me?"

He looks affronted. "I have a right to ask that question. She's my daughter."

"You have no rights. Not the right to breathe. To eat. To sleep. You can do *nothing* except what I let you do. That's what happened when she lost the game. Your life became mine."

"That's not real," he says, sputtering. "This isn't the Dark Ages."

"The Dark Ages. What a perfect description of the time we're living in."

"You can't own another person."

Then how does Penny have such a strong hold over me? Why do I worry about her with every inhale, hope for her happiness with every exhale?

If this isn't ownership, I don't know what it is.

"Give me your gloves," I say.

He looks down at his hands, clearly puzzled. I'm puzzled as well. Where does a grown man get gloves that look like they belong to a preschooler? He works it out in his head—the risks of defying me, the cost of obeying me. In the end he slowly takes off the knit gloves and hands them to me.

I take them in my bare hands, hands that have been pressed in a vice and burned on a stove. Hands that have done unspeakable violence.

"Where did you get these?"

"She gave them to me," he says, his voice raw. "They were a Christmas present a few years ago."

And cheap enough that he kept them all this time. If she got him anything worth enough to pawn, he would have already lost them. I examine them for a moment, feeling strangely detached. How would it feel to have something so warm? How it would feel to have something from her? She picked them out herself, paid for them with the pennies she made at the diner.

Then I open my fingers and watch them fall to the water's dark surface.

He doesn't say a word as his gloves sink to the bottom, their outline barely visible.

"You'll give me anything I tell you to," I say softly. "Including your daughter."

In the silence that follows, I can feel his struggle. The natural pride of a man, the instinctive protectiveness of a father. Both of those things rendered useless after what he did to her. I could have tied her to my bed, could have taken her a hundred thousand different ways.

And why didn't I? That's something I've asked myself a few times. Especially on cold days like this one, when I can feel every old scar and every old break. Why shouldn't I take relief where

I can find it?

Except for the memory of a little girl who loved to play with numbers the way other children play with dolls.

I move away from the railing, walking with a steady gait. One that doesn't have a limp. Very few people know that it exists. Only Gabriel Miller, actually. "You'll stay in Tanglewood," I say to the man struggling to keep up with me. "And you'll call her weekly."

"Weekly sounds good."

"I mean every week, not every other. Not once a month."

He makes a sound of protest. "Okay."

Most of the marks on my body, they were intended to hurt. Of course they would cause pain. It's the pain that made me stronger. Breathing through it. Fighting through it.

My father didn't want to do serious damage to my organs or my bones, the kind that would render me useless or dead. It was a kind of caring, how deliberate his abuse was.

Except when I traded myself for the girl. That was the only time I've ever seen him lose his temper, truly become angry instead of simply cruel. He beat me until I couldn't breathe, couldn't speak.

One particular blow of his boot to my back broke my hip bone.

He tossed me into an old well with a foot of water. He left me there for so many days that he must have wondered if I died. So many days that I wondered if he had taken the girl, after all.

"And whatever else happens, you won't speak of her to another living soul."

He looks at me, startled. "What? Why?"

Because she's like the limp in my step. The ache in my hands. The weakness in my body. "Because it's the only way to keep her safe."

CHAPTER ONE
PENNY

THE PILE OF textbooks in my small room grows and grows.

I live in a small room beneath the main floor, right next to the kitchens of a hotel. When the chef replaces their old-world chopping block with high-density polyethylene, I claim one of the slabs of wood from the discard pile. It's heavy enough that I need help to carry it to my room, turning it sideways through the door.

We put it on the textbooks, five stacks I've made to match in height. I use it as my desk, finding differentials over the scarred surface, solving proofs with the faint smell of cleaning solution and cilantro the wood can't quite relinquish.

With all these books, it's easy to think they have everything figured out. That only a few unsolvable problems remain in the realm of mathematics, a few edge cases to keep the modern academics engaged. Before I collect them I learn how limited they are.

Dr. Stanhope is my first professor at Smith College, relatively young for his tenure, with soft brown eyes and an uneven shave. He comes to class with ink staining his square-tipped fingers, which then become covered in white chalk. He's unlike any man I've known before, more of an alien creature than human, which makes him that much more relatable to me.

"Do we know all the math there is to know?" he asks on the first day. "Have we seen every arrangement of numbers there is to see? Have we seen every painting that will be painted?"

Because math, he explains, is more than just a discovery of natural laws. It's a creative endeavor, requiring basic knowledge but also ingenuity, curiosity, and an unquenchable search for new patterns in the real and abstract universe. It wakes in me a new understanding of myself—less of a machine, more of a woman with a heart. That my heart prefers order is maybe a result of my DNA or maybe a result of my chaotic childhood.

The class I take with him is the History of Mathematics, one of the only advanced-level courses available to me over the summer. I take that alongside Introduction to Calculus and

Sociology 101, unable to wait for the fall semester to begin.

I couldn't wait to be lost in numbers, but it's the people who capture me instead. Euler's feverish religious beliefs and his legendary "proof" of God. Turing's grand successes and subsequent persecution for his homosexuality, including a now banned hormonal treatment. Ada Lovelace, the only legitimate child of Lord Byron, who was the first person to recognize the potential of computers as more than pure calculation.

She described her approach as poetical science, which to me sounds perfect.

As the years pass I find more interest in literature and art than I ever had, as if the discovery of mathematics as a creative pursuit has given me permission. The numbers still call to me, as does Dr. Stanhope. He becomes my undergraduate advisor as I head into my junior year, both a mentor and a friend. A secret and painful crush, the kind of yearning for a life free from crime.

"Have you thought anymore about the research position?" he asks me in our weekly meeting, a cup of coffee in his hand, a book open on his lap as if he might dive into it at any point in our conversation. He cocks his head, the only sign that he's waiting for a response, his gaze trained on the book.

When we started meeting, we did so in his outer office, an ancient wood table with dusty cloth-covered chairs. The same place he would hold small tutoring sessions or where his research assistants might work. Later we moved to his inner office, him behind the imposing desk stacked high with books and loose paper, and me in the swivel chair in front of him.

Now we sit side by side on the plaid couch, more comfortable for the occasional academic debates we engage in. That's not a euphemism for anything, despite the images that sometimes invade my dreams. "I need to talk to my dad," I say, strangely reluctant to decide.

There is no future in a mathematics degree. It needs something practical to sit on top— engineering or computer programming. By itself it's about as useful as an art degree in terms of securing actual employment. Most everyone goes on to get their doctorate, which is what Dr. Stanhope expects me to do.

He even has a research position reserved for me, something both flattering and alarming. "Imagine how far you could go," he muses, looking at the bookshelves on the far end of the office, as if he can see the distance in his mind. He so rarely looks at me, directly at me, which has made it a comfort to talk to him. I still remember the direct silver gaze of a man intent on possessing me, consuming me; this abstract interest is so much safer.

"Of course I would love to," I say, anxious not to insult him. "The opportunity to work with you in-depth is incredible. And your last paper on quantitative bounds has so many possibilities for further research."

He smiles faintly. "Yes, I rather thought you would like that."

His particular focus is Ramsey problems, a rule concerning what price a monopolist should set in order to maximize social welfare. It's a unique intersection of human interest and mathematics, and something that makes him that much more honorable.

I fumble with my notebook, flipping to one of the last pages, my handwriting sharp in pen. "What you said about elasticity being unconstant, it made me think about the lower bounds. That there might be new methods to form them. I have this—well, it's only the beginning. But I think it's opened up a whole new door."

He takes the notebook from me and studies the numbers, that familiar little line of concentration between his eyes. "God, this is brilliant. I only sent you the final copy two days ago. You did this yesterday?"

"I could spend a lifetime on them," I say shyly.

He looks at me sideways. "Could you?"

"It's always been my dream to study. Not as a means to an end, as the end itself. But it's tricky with my home situation. I don't know whether I can afford to spend more time here."

A wave of his hand dismisses money as a concern. "A smart girl like you should never be barred from learning. I'm sure we can work something out."

Old worries wake up, cracking their eyes open as if from a long slumber. Memories of what men asked me to do at the seedy diner if I needed money. "Like what?"

"The usual. Grants. Financial aid. The research position pays a small amount, and should you be unable to cover the rest…" He closes the book with a snap that makes me jump. "I would be happy to help you myself."

A blush steals over my cheeks. "I don't think that would be appropriate."

He shrugs. "It's a flawed system, education. Favoring those who have money over those who have talent. I'm glad you found your way to Smith College, however it came about."

The oblique reference to my father's profession makes my cheeks turn hotter. He asked me once about my family, about what my father did for a living. I stammered something about how he worked for a businessman in Tanglewood, how I don't know exactly what he does.

Not a lie, precisely.

Damon Scott is a businessman, one who deals in flesh and crime.

And my father does work for him, in the way of some old-fashioned indentured servant, one unable to leave. What sort of *work* he actually does has always been secret, one I've never wanted to know, because it pays for my tuition here at school.

"I'm so glad, too," I say softly, because it's here that I became a woman.

I may have felt older than my years before, pretending I stood a chance in the urban jungle that was Tanglewood, lifting my chin to the black jaguar that was Damon Scott. Only coming here showed me what a wide world waits outside the city limits.

Only here did I learn that not every man wants you as his prey.

"I don't want to make you uncomfortable," he says, turning slightly toward me, and his words have the immediate opposite effect. I like him distracted and academic. I like him focused on something else. When he turns to look at me directly, it makes the air rush from my lungs. "But I do feel like I should say this before you make a decision. I see you as more than a student, Penny. Even more than a research assistant."

My lips form a shocked O, but I'm unable to speak.

"You're an uncommonly smart girl." He makes a wry expression, waving his hand at the books, some of which he's authored, at the proofs and calculations strewn around the office. "And I've made something of a life search for the singular and unique in this world, at least in the confines of dusty shelves. I think perhaps you're the best find I've ever had."

My heart pounds, hard and fierce, a drum of warning. But I can't help but be warmed by his words—*I think perhaps you're the best find I've ever had.* Coming from a man with multiple academic papers and accolades, and even a few patents to his name, it's a wild compliment.

"I'm not sure what to say."

He moves as if to touch my knee. It's something he's done before, but it takes on a new meaning as he reaches now. But he seems to catch himself, his hand hovering instead. "Only think about it," he says finally. "I know you're young. Younger than most students in your position."

It's been three years since I left Tanglewood for the first time. I'm nineteen now, but I feel more young than when I left. More aware of all the things I don't know. All the things I haven't done. Things like sex.

"I think of you as more than a professor," I tell him.

And like before, it's not quite a lie.

I do think of him in a sexual way, these strange and feverish thoughts that come to me at night. I think of him, having become a woman. I was just a child when Damon Scott visited me in my bedroom, when he held himself away from me. When he gave me my first kiss.

Professor Stanhope gives me a crooked smile, and I have a glimpse of the playboy he could have been had he a less focused mind. Handsome and intelligent and kind.

You'd be safe with me, that smile seems to say.

But I'm not sure I'm ready to resign myself to his dusty shelves, more an intricate proof than a partner, a cherished volume that he would run ink-stained fingers across. I would never go back to Tanglewood. There would be nothing left to hold me there. The thought brings a strange ache to my chest, as if I've lost something I can never get back.

CHAPTER TWO

I GET TO the Emerald late that evening, the sun streaking over sloping hills of dark moss. In the morning the sunlight will sparkle off the dew, which is what gave the house its name. Originally built as a vacation home for a powerful industrialist and a real-life Spanish princess, the house was eventually converted to a luxury hotel.

And then purchased by Gabriel Miller as an outright gift for Avery James.

A place for her to be safe and comfortable while she continues her graduate studies. A place for her to call home, to replace the one she lost. The hotel is still operational, only the top-floor penthouse reserved for Avery.

Gabriel still has a mansion in Tanglewood, but this is owned by her.

When I first came to Smith I lived in the dorm rooms with all the other freshman, but I have a hard time relating to the girls with their platinum credit cards and prep school backgrounds. Avery offered me permanent residence in one of the other suites, but that wouldn't feel right either.

Instead I started working in the kitchens and found a room reserved for on-site staff members. I'm much more comfortable among the waitstaff and line cooks and maids than I am upstairs.

I slip through the back door, past the bustle of the kitchen where Lorenzo shouts orders among the clamor of pots, past the steaming laundry room, into the dark narrow corridor. This used to be where servants slept, back when this was a single household. It's not so different now that I live and work in the kitchen part-time in exchange for rent.

I'm the modern-day servant, even if I am friends with the lady of the house. My cell phone buzzes as I drop my backpack on the twin-size bed. A text message from Avery. *Let me know when you're done. I want to go to the library.*

The Library isn't a place we go to study. It's a coffee shop by day, a bar by night. Basically where everyone hangs out when they aren't on campus or out clubbing. It's also a sweet compromise for when we want to loosen up, without actually joining the party scene.

I text her back. *Phone call tonight. I'll text*

when I'm done.

Then I flip open my notebook to keep working on the elasticity question, my phone faceup on the desk. For an hour I lose myself in linear equations and minimized surplus, finding comfort in the hard challenge of them, the struggle that always comes before revelation. In some ways it's not the solution I want, not the oasis; it's the mental test of endurance, a long trek through desert sands.

A knock comes at the door, startling me. I open it to reveal Avery, dressed in skinny jeans and a deep green cable-knit sweater that brings out her hazel eyes.

She frowns a little. "I was worried about you. The calls don't usually last this long."

I glance at the clock, my stomach clenching when I see the time. "He never called."

Ever since I left Tanglewood, ever since Daddy went to work for Damon Scott, he's called me every week like clockwork. As if it's part of his new job, and maybe it is. I wouldn't put it past Damon to keep tabs on me through him. Then again, that's probably pride talking. Maybe even perverse wishful thinking, because part of me wants to keep tabs on him.

But Daddy doesn't say much about it. I doubt

Damon has ever even asked him about me. Our conversations are short and tense, both of us holding back more than we're saying. He hasn't missed a phone call in three years. Even when he caught the flu last winter, he called, hoarse and miserable.

Some worry must show on my face, because she says, "We don't have to go out. I'm tired anyway."

Such a people pleaser, but her eyes couldn't be more clear. This girl isn't tired. She wants to go out. And why shouldn't she? For that matter, why shouldn't I?

"We're going," I say firmly, grabbing my phone. "I'll call him on the way."

I take a moment to look at myself in the dresser mirror, the brown eyes considerably more tired than Avery's, definitely more wary. The chapped lips and windburned cheeks. This is what Professor Stanhope saw? He really must be interested in my mind.

With a sigh I swipe some lip gloss so it looks like I didn't stumble in from a major exam, and drag my hair into a ponytail, which is a lazy version of dress-up hair. It falls down my back in shiny blonde curls as if I had anything to do with it.

Then I grab my coat and phone, pulling Avery along.

"I'll call Gabriel while you do yours," she says, falling beside me.

It's a fifteen-minute walk to the Library. We could use Avery's car and driver, but that takes almost as long through the heavy foot traffic around campus. Plus it's crazy conspicuous.

We head down the lit sidewalk, well-groomed flowers on both sides.

She pulls out her phone and hits speed dial while I do the same.

I put the phone to my ear. *Ring ring ring.* And then my father's voice: *It's me. Leave a message and I'll call you back.* It makes me smile because that's so much like him.

And then I frown. Something serious must be happening.

Don't freak out, I tell myself. Missing one call out of a hundred doesn't mean anything. His phone battery probably died or something like that. No big deal. I swipe the red circle to end the call.

Biting my lip, I contemplate my phone wallpaper, an abstract swirl of nothing.

I type a quick text before I shove the phone into my pocket. *Missed you. Call me when you can.*

It feels a little strange to even say that much. *Missed you.* Like I've revealed something unsavory. Like I've put ammunition in an enemy's hand. Maybe normal kids tell their father they love him. Maybe other dads say it back. We're anything but normal.

Avery's still on the phone. "We're going to have a drink. Some dinner." A pause. "Yes, at the Library. No, we didn't take the car."

I can hear a low sound, Gabriel's voice through the phone. Though I can't make out the words, I can guess what he's saying. *You shouldn't be walking alone at night.*

"I'm not alone," she says, proving my guess. "Penny's with me. There's safety in numbers."

There's safety in numbers.

Her words bounce around inside me, held inside by my skin, by every wish and hope and fear too real to name. That's what I've always believed, what I've always wanted to believe. The reason I should fall into Professor Stanhope's arms, no matter how inappropriate it might be.

Beyond the glow of the lamps, pitch-black night presses in. Anything could be out there. Anyone. I'm not sure we're safer in ones or in twos. I'm not sure we're safe at all.

CHAPTER THREE

B Y THE NEXT night I'm really worried about
Daddy, but I have to work. Lorenzo barks
out dishes as the room service orders come in.
Crab cakes and lobster rolls. Surf and turf.

A lone order for pancakes and grits comes in
around ten p.m., making me smile. That will be
Avery, having forgotten to eat dinner at a regular
hour, preferring some comfort food for a late-
night snack. Mostly I chop vegetables in large
quantities, refilling steel rectangular containers so
the line cooks can raid them. I also put garnishes
on the dishes with breakfast food and dessert,
turning strawberries into stars and beets into
accordions.

I spend an extra minute to turn the end of a
banana peel into a dolphin, its mouth holding a
plump blueberry like a ball. Lorenzo raises a stern
eyebrow at my creation, but he puts a silver dome
on the tray. And when he thinks I've looked away,
a small smile appears.

He's not an easy man to work for. I lived in terror that I was going to lose my job—and my home—when I first started working here. Then I stayed up all night studying for a chemistry exam. In my delirium I sliced open my finger while cutting zucchini. Lorenzo stormed over to me, and I thought, through the pain and exhaustion, *This is it. I'm fired.*

Instead, red-faced and cursing in Italian, he cleaned my wound himself, his rough knife-scarred hands gentle around mine. Ever since then he's been a hard-ass about making sure I don't work too much.

I finish refilling a deep well of chopped green onions and then wash my hands, one of fifty times I'll do that tonight. From experience I know that the scent will linger on my skin tomorrow. I'll pause between taking notes, my chin resting on my hand, and get a whiff of something fresh and green.

"Get out of here," Lorenzo growls, and I glance at the clock. Break time.

On another night I might tease him for worrying about me. Tonight I'm eager to take my break. I grab my phone from my work cubby and head outside. There's a small courtyard that would have been reserved for the servants—

modest by the old standards of mansions and royalty, but a luxury after the heat and clamor of the kitchens.

I sit on a cracked stone bench, pressing the speed dial.

It's me. Leave a message and I'll call you back.

This time I do leave a message. "Hey," I say, the sound of blood rushing blocking out my own voice. "It's me. You didn't call last night and... anyway, I worry about you. I understand if you're busy. Can you just drop me a quick text so I know you're okay?"

There are other questions caught in my throat. *What does Damon make you do for him? Is it dangerous? Of course it's dangerous. Do you hate me for putting you in this position?*

I hang up on dead air, staring into the night. "It's fine," I say into the quiet. "Everything is fine. His phone is probably broken. He's at the store getting it replaced right now."

With a leaden feeling in my stomach I return to the kitchen and complete the rest of my shift. It's a good thing that I mostly have to chop vegetables, because my hands can work without my mind. Lorenzo shouts at me once to pay attention, that I'm going to lose a pinky finger, but I end the night with all my appendages intact.

Only when I'm curled up in my bed after midnight do I turn on my phone again.

There's a text from a study partner about meeting up tomorrow. An e-mail from a professor about the exam next week. Nothing from Daddy. No return phone call. No text telling me he's okay.

Because he's not okay, a dark voice whispers inside me.

I should probably go to sleep. That's the rational thing to do. I can deal with this in the morning. And probably Daddy will have texted me by then. There's no reason to worry.

Except I find myself dialing the information line for Tanglewood.

"Damon Scott," I tell the robotic voice.

A digital sound and a pause, like a catch in her mechanical breath. Even the natural language processor knows I'm making a mistake. Then there's a ring, and another, before I have time to rethink what I'm doing. Miles away, over plains and mountains, across state lines. We're so far away, but he sounds like he's right next to me.

"Hello?" That low voice. That arrogance, that mystery.

There are years between us, a lifetime, but it might as well have been a minute. It all comes crashing back to me as I huddle on my twin bed, remembering the man who saved me, the man who stole me. The man who holds my father's life in his hands.

CHAPTER FOUR

IN THE SPACE between us there's a cool breeze, full of sweet memories and dark secrets, bringing with it the unique scent of boy and man. Everything that I tried so hard to forget, rushing back to me in a deep, soul-waking breath.

A fist tightens around my throat, but I don't know if it's in the shape of Damon Scott's hands. Am I afraid of him? Or am I afraid of who I am around him?

Silence stretches out in mocking accusation. *Afraid, afraid, afraid.*

"Penny," he says on a sigh that sounds almost obscene, so carnal and pleased.

I'm no longer a sixteen-year-old girl, even if I feel like it right now. "Where's my father, Damon?"

There. I spoke in an even tone, not tripping over the words. No tremor to match how I'm feeling inside. It's a testament to years spent around young women like Avery, most of them raised with good breeding and high-society manners. The kind who have their picture in the newspaper after a night at a charity gala. I can pretend, even if that will never be me.

His rough laugh obliterates all my grand ideas. "Is that how you say hello? You don't call. You don't write. If I were inclined to that sort of thing, I might think you didn't care about me."

"He works for you. That means you know where he is."

"Then he's probably busy. He must be, for what I pay him."

"Every Wednesday he calls me. And now nothing."

"How much *do* I pay him?" he asks, his voice thoughtful. "I'll have to check the books to be sure, but it must be a lot. Enough to cover your private college tuition."

I flinch, glad he can't see me across two thousand miles. Even working in the kitchens most nights only covers my food, my textbooks. Not the tuition bill. "You're the one who wanted him to work for you. You're the one who made him the stake in our last game."

"And you're the one who lost," he says lightly.

"Do you know where he is?"

"Of course. Like you said, he works for me. I

would be a careless employer if I let my men go wandering off, gambling and racking up debt and questioning their loyalty to me."

A shiver runs through me. "Then where is he?"

"He's a grown-up, Penny. Like you are now. He's responsible for himself. You only need to worry about your studies. I'm sure Algebraic Topology is taking up plenty of your focus."

It's one of my courses this semester. How does he know that?

"Stop playing with me."

"Why should I?" he says with a soft laugh. "It's so much fun."

Frustration stings my eyes, hot and damp. I look up at the wide-open sky, willing myself not to cry. There are a million stars visible here, most of the land owned by Smith College or one of the other campuses. So much land, so much pride. There aren't buildings climbing on top of other buildings, as if they might sink into the concrete ground if they don't. There aren't glass towers reaching to an endless black sky.

"I'm never coming back," I say abruptly.

His laugh falls silent. "I know."

"I hate it there. I hate Tanglewood and being powerless. And most of all I hate you."

The last part is a lie, because I don't hate him. I'm drawn to him; I'm repelled by him. It's far too complex a relationship, an equation I've never been able to write. It makes me wonder if I'm lying about the other parts—if maybe some twisted part of me misses home.

If some twisted part of me misses being powerless, too.

"Ah, Penny," he says, sounding infinitely weary. "I hate you too."

The words shock me, but the hurt inside shocks me more. He shouldn't be able to wound me. Three years away from home, growing up, growing strong. It should have been enough armor to protect against anything he could say to me. But the arrow sinks deep, proving that I'll never be able to escape him.

"What did I do to you?" I ask, quiet, in a voice like I'm six years old again. Like I'm speaking to the wild boy I found by the lake, one I lured into my trailer like a wolf.

He answers the same way, a surly teenage boy, fierce and vulnerable at once. "You made me care. You made me want, when I needed to leave. You made me feel, when I would have preferred to die. You brought me back to life."

And I condemned him to torture. That's what

happened when he sacrificed himself so that I could stay safe. Two children with so few choices. "I'm sorry," I whisper.

"Don't worry. I got my revenge, after all."

My blood runs cold, almost subzero at the words. There's only one person left in my sad little family. One person he could hurt. "Did you hurt him?"

"By giving him a job when he couldn't hold one down? By paying him enough that his daughter could escape the city, could go to a fancy college instead of becoming a corner-store whore? Yes, I've been horrible to him. A monster."

"Then why isn't he answering his phone?"

In the pause I can picture him in a three-piece suit, reclining in one of his ridiculously expensive leather chairs. Some amber liquid in a crystal-cut glass. "Don't come back," he says, his voice grim. "You made it out of here. Let that be enough."

A soft *click* ends the connection, leaving me bereft.

And more worried than before.

Something is happening in Tanglewood, something bad enough for my father not to call, something horrible enough that even Damon Scott has warned me away. I look up at the infinite stars, but they're dimmer than before. The whole world muted. It wasn't a new life that I found so far from home. It was a long dream, and now I'm painfully awake.

CHAPTER FIVE

I GO TO class the same way, trying to pretend nothing is wrong. And it's not that hard, because I've gone numb. The worn wood of the desks doesn't register beneath my hands. The chatter of other students around me can't make its way through thick cotton.

Calculating projective spaces in my Algebraic Topology class doesn't hold my attention. I write down random numbers, draw random lines and spheres. My mind is filled with nothingness, as bleak and oppressive as the Tanglewood sky. *Don't come back,* Damon told me, but it feels like I'm already there. In mind if not in body.

I don't have an advisory session scheduled with Dr. Stanhope today, but I have to pass by his office after class. Usually I'd head to the commons for lunch, maybe meet up with Avery for a cup of coffee after. Instead I find myself knocking on his door.

"Come in," he says in that absent way of his,

but even that doesn't bring me comfort today.

He glances up from his work, then gives me a double take. Do I look that bad? The concerned line between his brows says yes. "Sit down, Penny."

Without waiting for me to respond, he guides me gently to the sofa. His touch is confident, firm, the kind I can rely on, and right now I'm desperate for someone to hold me.

Even if he's not the man I'm dreaming about.

From my seat on the old plaid couch I study Dr. Stanhope as if for the first time. Soft brown eyes and a strong jaw. He has the kind of hair that's deep mahogany, that would turn to golden if he spent more time in the sun. It's cut short, I'm sure because that requires the least amount of thought on his part.

His shirt is a rumpled white, probably one of ten exactly like it hanging in his closet. Black slacks and brown loafers, which don't quite match but somehow fit this man.

"Something's wrong," he says softly, a gentle nudge.

I take a deep breath. "I'm not sure it's right for me to talk about this with you."

My professor. My mentor. And what else? The man who wants me. A faint smile touches his lips, as if he's thinking the same thing. "I can be your friend."

"I thought you wanted to be something else."

"Lovers are friends," he says softly.

Not the way Damon Scott does it. "I'm worried about my dad."

Brown eyes sharpen, the same as when he's faced with a new puzzle. "What happened?"

"I don't know. Maybe nothing." Each word drags from me, my long-held privacy creating friction on the way out. How can I bare my soul to Dr. Stanhope, to anyone? Then again it's not my soul that's being exposed. Only my sordid past. "But he didn't call me like he usually does. And he's not answering his phone."

"Do you have someone else you could call?"

Someone else. Other family. Friends. Isn't that what normal people have?

I could call Brennan but I haven't spoken to him for three years. We broke up unceremoniously when I left for Smith College, both of us understanding that I had chosen a life outside Tanglewood—and that it could never include him.

"We don't know that many people," I admit slowly. "I called the diner where I used to work. My friend Jessica works there. At least, she used to. I called this morning. She's gone."

He frowns. "Gone, as in she quit?"

"As in she didn't show up for work one morning. Another girl stopped by her apartment a week ago. The door was kicked in. No trace of Jessica or her baby."

"Damn," he mutters softly. "A baby? Did they call the police?"

I flush, uncertain how to explain the lawless city I come from, that Jessica may have run from the cops themselves. "It's complicated, but I'm afraid something is wrong. I have to go home."

"Do you want me to come with you?"

My mouth falls open. The offer stuns me. I can't imagine showing Dr. Stanhope the dark streets of Tanglewood, but the prospect of having help steals my breath. "You would do that?"

He smiles a little, self-deprecating. "I must have done a worse job communicating than I thought. I care about you, Penny. Deeply. I would do a lot for you. Probably more than bears mentioning."

Two men saying they care about me in a twenty-four hour period is more than my heart can take. After a lifetime of wanting only one person to care, two is too many. "We're in the middle of a semester."

One eyebrow rises, as if he's surprised I'm considering it. "That's the benefit of tenure. I can take an emergency absence."

"Am I an emergency?" I ask faintly.

"Since the first time you raised your hand in my class."

My mind shifts through the entry-level class. What did I raise my hand to ask? I'm embarrassed at how naive I must have been, fresh out of Tanglewood and thinking I knew everything. "It must have been ridiculous."

He shakes his head, not really denying it—more like he's still stunned by me, three years later. "You had the most perfect explanation of string theory I've ever heard. Not only from an undergraduate. From PhDs on the subject. But you didn't know how to access the syllabus."

Humiliation burns in my chest. I had barely ever used the Internet. There was a computer lab in my high school, but the roof had leaked, and it had been closed the whole time I went there. Then I had taken my GED to get out early. It had felt too much like a farce to sit down and pretend not to know anything after I had seen the devil himself.

When I got a perfect score on the SATs, Avery and Gabriel pulled some strings so Smith College would look at me. When I scored the ninety-ninth percentile on their admissions test, they let me in.

"I don't know how you didn't laugh at me," I say, cheeks flaming.

"God, Penny. I wish you could see yourself like I do."

I turn my face away, unable to look at him. Unable to have him look at me. How does he see me? He catches my chin and turns me toward him. My eyelids must weigh a thousand pounds. I can't raise my gaze to meet his. Not until he lifts me from the couch, pulling me onto his lap.

I'm too stunned to protest. I look at him, shocked and strangely excited. His brown eyes are darker than usual, still soft, but with desire now.

And there's something hard pressing against my hip.

"What are you doing?" I whisper.

"Nothing yet," he says softly, tucking my hair behind my ear. "You looked like you needed someone to hold you."

A shudder runs through my body, a visceral reaction to his words. I need someone to hold me, desperately. I need *him* to hold me. "I'm not who you think I am."

"Then who you are?" he asks, his expression

tender.

I'm the girl who's saying goodbye. "Where I grew up, it's not like here. It's dangerous. Daddy is mixed up in something bad. And it might be my fault."

"Is it?" His voice is thoughtful. "Or do you want it to be?"

The question rings in my ears long after I leave his office.

CHAPTER SIX

"TELL ME TO stay," I ask Avery, almost desperate for her to convince me. "Tell me to stay at Smith College, to ignore what's going on at home, to do whatever I have to do to finish here."

"Is that what you want to do?" she asks quietly.

We're in her penthouse suite, curled up on the antique sofa with a plush throw blanket and a bucket of popcorn. I've already put in my formal request to take a leave of absence and booked the flight for tomorrow. Which makes this goodbye.

"I don't have a choice," I say, though we both know that isn't true.

A haunted expression crosses her pretty face. She always looks so put together. Even in class her nails are perfectly shaped and her lip gloss in place. Her makeup is never overdone, but it's definitely polished. Only when she's in her suite does she let her guard down.

"Look, I want to support you. Especially with how hard this must be. But I feel like I should say… you *can* stay. You *should* stay. Your father is your past. This is your future."

"Is that what *you* would do?"

"No," she admits ruefully. "I would have done anything for my father. And I guess I did. I can't say that I really regret it, but it also was misguided. I was blind to his faults. So desperate to hold on to my last piece of family."

Acid burns my throat. "I know what that's like."

"The women in Tanglewood don't fare too well," she says softly.

I know the sad story of her mother, how even with all her money and education she hadn't managed to escape the dark side of the city. It would be even harder without those resources. Impossible. It had been pure luck that had let me leave the first time.

That luck won't find me again.

"I don't think I can stay here, knowing he might be in trouble. But I don't want to leave. It's been too good here," I say in a whisper, a little rueful. To know what it's like, life without struggling for my next meal, for the next five dollars that may never come.

"You can come back," Avery says.

She's a wonderful friend, but she doesn't know what it's like to be hungry for years. And I wouldn't wish that on her. "Maybe."

"You can," she insists. "You can visit home, make sure your dad is okay, and then fly back. If you need money, I can help."

"Please," I say, my cheeks turning warm. "You've done enough for me."

She frowns. "It's not charity, Penny. You're my friend."

"And you're my friend. That's why I don't want to take advantage of you."

This is an argument we've had before. I can see the old arguments in the air of her apartment, how she *wants* to help me, how she doesn't need the money. It feels too good to have a friend, though. One I don't owe. One who doesn't owe me.

"It's not only that," I admit. "I'm a little afraid to go home. To see *him.*"

She doesn't ask who I mean. Damon Scott. The man who saved me. The man who pushed me away. And the only person who will know where Daddy is.

"Do you think he'll give you a hard time?" she says, sounding worried, as if *she* thinks he'll give me a hard time. "I can ask Gabriel to talk to him. He's out of the country at the moment, but—"

"No, it's not that. It's more about my reaction to him."

"Oh," she says knowingly.

"I think I was silly before. Thinking there was anything between us. He's probably forgotten all about me." This is what I convinced myself. It was the only way I could actually leave Tanglewood. After the phone call I'm not so sure.

But even if he cared about me back then, I was a little girl. How could he have cared about me? How could he have *known* me? I barely even knew myself. The young woman sitting on this couch with Avery James is someone else entirely.

"Or maybe he's been pining after you."

My throat gets tight, filled with words I don't dare say. "No. I was only a teenager when I saw him last. He kissed me, but I think… I'm afraid it was only out of pity."

She looks dubious. "I don't think Damon Scott kisses people out of pity."

"Maybe not. But it's been three years. He could have kissed every girl in the city by now."

"He could have kissed none of them."

Only when my heart beats faster do I realize that's what I've been wishing for. How stupid of me. How presumptuous. And yet I can't deny the possibility. He *had* kissed me. And it hadn't felt like pity, the faint tremor in his strong body, the gentle way his lips touched mine.

"Has Gabriel said anything about him lately?"

Avery's hazel eyes grow troubled. "No, but I'm not sure if he would tell me. They've been arguing. And he's been gone so much for work. So much traveling."

There's more than travel bothering her. I feel her unease as surely as my own, dark and sinewy, climbing our ankles like vines. "Have you told him you're worried about him?"

Her nose scrunches. "I shouldn't be surprised you can see right through me. You always were crazy smart."

"With numbers," I remind her. "Not people."

"They're not so different, I think. Both of them are puzzles."

I put her hand in mine. "I can tell you're worried because I care about you."

It still feels strange to touch anyone.

I didn't get hugged much as a child. My mother left early, first in spirit, losing herself in drugs and men. Then in body. Daddy did his best for me, but he was never much of a hugger. Maybe that's why it meant so much for Damon

Scott to hold me. He was really the first person who did.

She squeezes my hand, looking grateful. "I didn't want to tell anyone. Not even him. As if saying the words would make it more real. I can't help but think one of these days he's going to go away and not come back."

My blood runs cold. That's the dream I had since I was a child. One by one, everyone I love disappearing. Like a terrible fable, one that ends with me alone.

I struggle to keep my voice even. "You should tell him how you feel."

"No, he would just worry about me. Maybe even stay here more when he really needs to be visiting to make these deals. I know I should feel better that he's had this rift with Damon Scott. He's mostly a criminal. Definitely dangerous. That leaves Gabriel with more time to focus on his legitimate business."

Definitely dangerous. The words echo in my head. "But?"

"But it was good to know someone had his back. At least they trust each other. Or they did. Now it seems like everyone has some secret agenda. And Gabriel is operating by himself."

"He probably has a good sense of who to

trust. That's how he got so far."

"You're right," she says, smiling a little. It's troubled, though. She's not convinced. And the truth is, neither am I. It bothers me more than I want to admit to hear that Gabriel Miller and Damon Scott have had a falling out. What could it be about?

"Things will seem better in the morning," I say, not because I believe it but because I want it to be true.

Worry draws a crease between her eyebrows. "Will you sleep over?"

"Oh." I glance at the large California king, covered in plush white 1000-thread count linens. It's definitely big enough for the both of us, but still weird to be where Gabriel would sleep.

"Come on," she says, her voice teasing. "You're way too drunk on popcorn and Perrier to walk back to your room." Her tone grows serious. "And I'm actually kind of scared to be alone."

That decides me. "Of course I'll stay. And tomorrow you'll call Gabriel and tell him what you're really feeling. He deserves to know, and you deserve to have him help you through it."

"Yes, ma'am," she says, relief in her voice.

I feel relieved too, to not sleep alone for one night out of a thousand, to have a break from the dreams that plague me. But the nightmares come again, worse than ever. I'm in a crowd of glittering diamonds and gold, so sparkling I can't even see anyone's faces. And then one by one the lights go out. The people disappear. Until I'm left standing alone in a ballroom.

And then the ballroom turns into an empty pool, its green tiles cracked, dark roots breaking it apart from underneath. It's filling with water, blackness rising, until I can't see anything at all.

Chapter Seven

I WAKE UP startled, as if I had been falling in my dream, arms jerking back to catch my fall. The bed where I land is warm and soft—and very, very big. It's not clear for two minutes, three, that I'm alone in it. The piles of pillows don't hold anyone but me.

Sheets cling to my damp skin as I sit up in bed, blinking at the wide empty space. My room is the size of an ordinary dorm room, and I like that about it. It's small. And it's mine.

This room belongs to Avery James, who is basically modern-day royalty. Antique furniture and artwork tastefully decorate the large space. On the far coffee table I see the half-empty popcorn bowl we left and a couple of green glass water bottles. The teal scales on my phone case glitter in the morning light. Pushing away the heavy down comforter, I get out of bed and stumble across the room.

The phone blinks low battery at me, having

sat here all night without charging.

The time is ten o'clock, way later than I usually wake up. I got used to rising early working at the diner back home. Sleeping until eight when I get up for class still feels like a luxury.

"Avery?" I ask out loud. My voice seems to echo back at me.

I glance at the bathroom, where the door sits half-open, the claw-foot bathtub dark and dry. Maybe she went downstairs to talk to the staff for some reason. She does own the hotel, even if she doesn't usually get involved in operations.

Or maybe Gabriel came home early and surprised her.

Then why didn't I wake up and hear him? And where did they go? It would be just like Avery to not want to wake me. They could have found an empty hotel room on a lower floor and left me to sleep.

The more I think about it, that must be what happened. I certainly hope that's what happened. Because Avery has been so worried about him. I can't imagine her relief to have him safely home.

Something buzzes faintly in the room, and I turn back toward the bed. It's coming from the mountain of white sheets and blankets. I pull aside pillows, letting them fall to the floor like I'm excavating something. And the results of my dig are a phone, this one with a pink and black Kate Spade phone case that I recognize as being Avery's. Why would she leave her suite without her phone?

On the screen I can see Gabriel Miller, his stern expression and golden eyes startling.

For a brief moment relief lightens my chest. I can imagine how it played out—a middle-of-the-night text from Gabriel, Avery taking the elevator down to meet him, both of them so giddy to be together they found the first empty room to be alone.

And then in the morning, wondering where her phone went. Gabriel calling it to see if it rings in their temporary room. It makes perfect sense in my head, so sweet it makes me smile.

That's how I answer the phone—smiling.

"This is Avery's phone speaking."

Static bounces back at me. "Hello? *Avery?*"

I recognize Gabriel Miller's growl of a voice even with the bad connection. And his concern comes through loud and clear. My skin prickles. *Someone walking on your grave.* That's what Mama would say. But I'm more concerned with Avery than me. "Gabriel? This is Penny."

A crackle, more interference than sound.

"Where are you? Is Avery with you?"

There's a touch of relief in his voice, as if he's glad to have reached me, as if he's sure that I'll answer, *yes, she's right here.* As sure as I'd been that everyone was okay when I picked up the phone.

"No," I say, my voice almost hushed. The situation seems that serious. The luxe penthouse suite suddenly seems that sinister. "I'm in her suite. I spent the night, but when I woke up, she was gone."

He curses in a long and foul string, punctuated by crackles and snaps of the phone line. "Are there any calls last night on her phone?"

Putting the call on speaker, I flip through her iPhone until I get to the recent calls. "Looks like something came in at 1:35 a.m. last night. Or this morning, I guess. A missed call."

"That was me at the airport." Gabriel mutters. "What's after that?"

"There's nothing else."

So where did she go? And why didn't I wake up when she did? I was only a foot away from her in bed, but probably too exhausted from a full course load and working in the kitchen to hear her leave. Guilt eats at my throat like acid.

He swears again. "I'll call Professor Wilson. Can you look around the Emerald?"

Professor Anna Wilson is her graduate advisor and close friend, after they went to a Greek excavation together this past summer. I can't imagine why Avery would have gone to campus on a random Saturday morning, without her phone, leaving me sleeping in her room. There aren't really mythology research emergencies. But if she went anywhere near Smith College, Professor Wilson would know about it.

"I'll ask my manager," I promise. "We'll find her."

My mind is still a little sluggish from sleep. I might have thought I drank too much alcohol if we'd had any at all. Waking up in a new place, finding my friend mysteriously gone—it's all leaving me disoriented. I struggle for good reasons she might have left and come up empty.

"Gabriel," I say slowly. "Why did you know to call this morning?"

It filters in, the flick of a lightbulb, that he had been worried when he first called. That he has a terrible connection, but he still knew to find her. *He knew she might be missing.*

He's silent for one beat, two.

Long enough for horrible possibilities to fill the empty space in my mind.

"We talked yesterday," he says, which doesn't

answer the question. "She told me about your father."

It's that feeling I have when I'm on the right track with a proof, more instinct than logic. I know there are intellectual cogs working in the background, connecting clues before I can formulate the numbers on paper. Or say the words out loud. But right in this moment it feels more like intuition.

Two people missing. "Do you think they're connected?"

"No," he says, but I'm not sure I believe him.

The slap of muscle against bone, my heart pumping in wild expansion. "I don't understand how they could be connected. I talked to her last night before we went to sleep. She even told me I should stay here and wait it out. That I shouldn't leave."

"She's right," he says. "You should stay there."

But it doesn't sound like agreement. It's more like a warning.

I press my palm to my forehead, feeling like the penthouse is spinning. Or maybe it's just me. "Tell me what happened. You must have found something. Something to make you worry about her. What was it?"

"Ask everyone at the hotel if they've seen her.

Pull them out of bed if you have to. And call me the second you hear anything, understand? I'll be on the first flight there, but still call me. I'll make it work."

"Gabriel."

He makes a hoarse sound. "I always worry. Ever since…"

Ever since we found out that her biological father had stalked her and hurt her. The same man who assaulted me. Except Jonathan Scott is dead, isn't he? He's not a threat anymore. So why do I still feel afraid?

There are bands around my chest. One for memory and one for fear. And another for watching my future crumble. There's no pretending nothing is wrong. No Dr. Stanhope and the impossible dream of a different life. The roots of the city run way too deep to really let me go.

CHAPTER EIGHT

I STEP OUT of the cab, blinking at the bright lights shining from the Den's windows. Pavement pulses with a life of its own, the music from inside its heart. I paid the driver twenty bucks extra to wait while I ran inside Daddy's apartment, but it was empty. Not a surprise considering he isn't answering his cell. My stomach still sinks to the bottom of my feet, my whole body jittery and hot.

I've been this way since I found Avery gone, half-wondering if I'll wake up.

If all of this is just a dream.

The Den is a private club for the rich and dangerous men of Tanglewood. I've seen the place dark, almost abandoned, with Damon in a half-buttoned shirt and no shoes. And I've seen the place glittering like an underground casino prepared for the biggest game of the city.

But I've never seen it look like a nightclub, purple and blue and pink pressing against the windows, smoke winding out of the narrow opening in the door. Two large men wearing black T-shirts stretched across muscle guard the door, a seedier version of the lions who guard fancy libraries. Patience. Fortitude. And a flat aspect in their eyes that makes me uncomfortable.

I drag my carry-on luggage behind me, thumping down the stone steps to the landing, the door below street-level. The iron railing is slick with dew, because it's closer to dawn than midnight. The roar behind the heavy oak door shows no signs of stopping.

"Hello," I shout over the noise. "I'm here to see Damon Scott."

One bouncer looks at me, unimpressed. The other doesn't even bother to look away from that place two feet in front of his face. Neither of them make a move to let me in. They don't move to stop me, either.

"Can I go inside?"

The bouncer who acknowledged me gives a noncommittal nod. Apparently they aren't very concerned with a guest list at this party. Or security, considering anything could be in this luggage.

What on earth is going on?

I step through the door, half expecting them

to spring into action and block me. But I stumble into the dimly lit foyer, the mirror reflecting the light of a disco ball that appears to have been slung from the antique chandelier with rope.

My eyes struggle to adjust as I stumble over something blocking the path. It's one of the leather chairs, I realize. The ones that normally sit in uneven circles around the gilt tables, for men to have dangerous thoughts. Now it's sideways in the hallway.

And it's moving.

In a flash of scattered purple light I see why. There are two people on the other side, half-naked, having sex. Or very, very close. They're moving in rhythm with the music, making the chair undulate against me, almost as if they're grinding directly on me.

I jump back and bump into another group of people in the opposite parlor. Not dancing. They're kissing. They're doing a lot more than kissing—having sex in a tangle of limbs and tongues. God, what's happening here?

I feel like I've fallen through the mirror and ended up in some alternate version of Tangle-wood, everything turned around and upside down. Daddy is missing, and now there's some kind of orgy happening at the Den. Maybe

Damon Scott is missing, too.

Or maybe he's been pining after you.

Avery's voice rings in my ears. What if he withdrew from the Den? From a life of crime?

He might not even realize what's happening in this place, how they've torn it apart.

I push farther into the Den, determined to find the stairs. I know which bedroom is Damon's, a fact that still brings heat to my cheeks despite all the sinful acts being performed around me.

Through the doorway I can see a dance floor, where a crush of people move to the music that seems to emanate from the walls. I have one foot on the stairs, the heavy little luggage lifted an inch off the hardwood floor, when I see something in the far corner of the dance floor.

A little space carved out of the crowd, an invisible velvet rope respected by these people who've respected nothing else in the Den.

I take one step closer, drawn by the mystery of it, the gravity.

And there's Damon Scott, sitting in a high-backed leather chair, a devilish half smile on his face, two days growth shadowing his jaw. His suit is past rumpled, as if he's worn it several days now, but he shows no sign of slowing. Dark eyes survey the crowd like a man looking out over his land—and in a way, that's what these people are. The valleys and hills of his inheritance, fertile ground being sown.

In the opposite corner I can see a bell-shaped black-iron cage, six feet tall, with a woman dancing inside. Another one, taller, rectangular, has a muscular man wearing a thong and a collar. Their expressions are as blissed-out as the people dancing around them, despite the hands reaching through the bars to touch oiled skin—or maybe because of them.

Something small and pink withers inside me. It seems ludicrous to think that he would have pined after me. That he thought about me at all. I must have seemed like a child to him, whether my body had been grown-up or not—as innocent and foolish as a child.

It makes my crush on him that much more humiliating.

And it makes my presence here ridiculous. What did I think would happen? That I would find him lonely and halfway in love with me? That I would demand answers and he would give them? That he would magically produce Avery and then confess how much he missed me?

Half-naked women aren't dancing on his lap,

but it's close. They're near him, showing off bodies in lace and satin and leather. The kind of women you see on TV and magazines, too beautiful to be real. People say that there's an epidemic of Photoshop in the media, but these women aren't airbrushed. They're moving with confidence and glamour and unabashed sexiness.

While I stand in the hallway wearing yoga pants, my hair in a rough ponytail.

I don't know how long I would have stood there, debating with myself, hating myself, but Damon glances up. His eyes meet mine. For a moment I see a storm inside them—regret, anger. Accusation. It chills me to the bone, wind lashing me from twenty feet away.

Then he stands, and I taste something new. Metallic. *Fear.*

I don't know the man walking toward me. My dreams cast him as the savior. My nightmares showed his father as the devil. But those were the imaginings of a little girl, the same as my terrible crush and my private yearning.

The crowd parts for him, some without even looking back. They feel his energy as strongly as I do, pulsing as if the beat emanates from him. Smoke rises up around him, behind him, framing him in such a demonic light that I know I feared the wrong man.

He stops in front of me, casual, expectant.

And I find myself filling the space between us. "I'm looking for my dad. I didn't realize you were having a party. He wasn't at home. I can wait until you're... done."

That makes him smile. "Will you wait for me?"

What if he waited for you?

My cheeks turn hot. I must be bright red from shame. Can he guess what I dreamed about? Because whether I meant to or not, I have been waiting for him. Living my life in books, in numbers on paper, the smell of wood shavings and chalk in my nose. There haven't been dates. Not even many friends.

I have been waiting for this man, the illusion of him. Someone who doesn't exist.

"No," I tell Damon Scott. "We need to talk. Right now."

CHAPTER NINE

THE CROWD FALLS quiet, attuned to us in a matter of seconds.

Not because he spoke to me. That earned me resentful glances or mild curiosity. What brings the room to a halt is my disobedience, as if I've disrupted the entire flow of the party by fighting back. The beat of the music still thrums around us, heavy vibrations on the taut crowd.

I can hear the jangle of iron chains from someone shackled to the corner, eyelids heavy as they watch me, hips still thrust upward in a gyration never completed. I can hear the slick sound of skin against skin as the tangle on the fallen-over armchair twist to look at me. A cold giggle from one of the girls who'd been dancing near Damon before he came over.

God, even the silence here is hedonistic and cruel.

"I'm listening," he says, cool and sharp as a blade.

He listens with his whole body, his tall frame relaxed and expectant, his eyes hooded. The rest of the room is listening, too. This is better entertainment than half-naked people dancing in a cage. Than people having sex in a fallen-over leather armchair. This is the show.

"Well," Damon says in that showman's voice. As if he's the ringmaster, the Den his human circus. "If you have something to say, go ahead and say it. We can't wait to hear."

Every pair of eyes in the Den swings looks at me. I can smell the sex and the sweat in the air, feel the heavy breathing from all around. "I'd like to talk in private."

"Would you?" Damon says, circling me. "You don't look like you have much to bargain with."

I'm painfully aware of my slouchy travel clothes, my old ballet flats, the frayed carry-on that I found at a thrift store for five dollars. His dark eyes take me in, all of me, from my appearance to my worry, the fear that I've lived in since I woke up in Avery's empty bed days ago.

"It's a serious matter," I say, proud that my voice doesn't waver. There are a hundred people looking at me right now, each one of them more experienced than me.

And then there's Damon himself, their dark

king. Benevolent. Capricious.

Both a powerful leader and the disruptive force.

His voice is mocking now. "A serious matter? You better tell me fast, then."

There aren't any words in my head. All the things I'd planned to say to him—*where's my father? Where's Avery? What have you done to them?*—evaporated in the face of his scorching derision.

"Have you lost a puppy, little girl?" A laugh spreads through the crowd, as tactile as the groping hands and shining skin that undulated to the music minutes ago. "Or maybe you *are* the lost little puppy. Have you lost your owner?"

The worst part is that his words make me feel like a lost animal, wandering the streets, desperate for someone to take me in. With my father's empty apartment fresh in my memory and my second-hand luggage, it's not very far from the truth.

I look around at the people gawking, at their delight in my discomfort. They think they know what Damon Scott will do. They think they know him, but I knew the boy before he became a man. I saw him lanky and determined. I watched him trade his own safety to protect me.

"Where's my dad?"

That earns me a small smile, his lids low. "Does he tell you about his day when he calls you? About threatening people for money? About following through?"

Acid burns my throat, because Daddy never mentions that. And I'm not naive enough to think it hasn't happened. When I'm at one of the best colleges in the country, while I live in that dreamworld of numbers and Greek symbols, he's doing dirty work for a dangerous criminal king.

"So where is he now?"

An indolent shrug of one shoulder. "I haven't seen him. Though I did hear through the grapevine that he started gambling again." He makes a *tsk* sound. "That's never a good thing. Once debts start to pile up, how can I trust him to be loyal? I can't."

My blood runs cold. "Did you do something to him?"

"Let's be clear, sweetheart. Whatever happened to him, he did it to himself." The cold silver of his eyes tells me Damon's conscience would not ache for even one second over my father's death.

"You asshole," I hiss, unable to hide my anger any longer.

A man steps forward, someone I've never seen before. He's wearing a suit that's been undone in most of the ways it can be, rumpled and pushed aside. I barely have time to register his aggression, his instinctive response to my insult. How does a man obtain that kind of blind loyalty?

The man reaches for me, his fingers brushing my wrist.

That's how close he gets before everything shatters. Damon moves so fast he's a blur. When he stills, he has the man pressed against the wall, arm twisted at a strange angle.

"No one touches her." Damon's voice is quiet, but it carries through the crowded hall.

A rustle moves through the crowd, half awareness, half movement. The way they look at me has changed, the hostility faded away, replaced by something else. Maybe deference. Or fear.

I'm under Damon Scott's protection now. That's what he's just made clear.

He steps away from the man, leaving him writhing in pain against the wall.

"I didn't kill your father," he says, his voice low enough to be private. What I requested before, if not quite the way I wanted. "I haven't seen him in weeks. He's not here."

It's a dismissal, one that I should be grateful

for. And if it were only my father, I would leave. I would search the old gambling spots where he used to lose his paychecks. I would find new ones.

Except it's not only my father at stake here.

"What about Avery?"

Damon Scott doesn't suck in a breath. He doesn't widen his eyes or make any kind of movement that might be perceived as weakness. He had those reactions beaten out of him a long time ago. There's only a blade where a man might have stood, cool and silver and sharp. "What about her?"

"She's your sister. Don't you care that she's missing?"

"How long?"

I know Avery said Gabriel and Damon had a falling out, but how could they not have spoken about this? They were business partners once. Friends in that way that only predators could be, more of a truce and a reserved respect than actual affection. "I can't believe he didn't tell you."

"How long?" he repeats, his voice even.

"Seven days." My heart clenches hard as I say the words aloud. The reality of the situation sinks in more in that moment than before. I can no longer imagine this is a dream. No longer hope she's pulling some extended surprise vacation.

This is happening. "We talked to the police. To campus security. It's like she vanished. Gabriel flew there that day and tore the place apart. He's still there, looking."

And he isn't sleeping or eating. He looks like a tornado hit him.

For a while I stayed there, too, hoping we'd find her on campus or in the Emerald. Only when it became clear that she wasn't anywhere did I have to leave. And I felt a pull toward Tanglewood, as if the answers would be here.

Is it a coincidence that my father and Avery went missing so close together? They really have nothing in common, except for me. In that way they're parts of the same puzzle. Variables in the same equation. I have to solve this. That's the only way to bring them back. It's the only way to find them both. The only way to make sure I don't disappear as well.

CHAPTER TEN

PRESIDENTS RUN FOR office. Dictators steal it. Kings are born, and that's why it's the perfect way to describe Damon Scott. He commands any room he enters. He owns the very ground he walks on. And he wears that invisible crown with both pride and resignation, because it's a bittersweet birthright.

Jonathan Scott ruled the west side of Tanglewood through terror. Everyone knew not to cross him, even a six-year-old girl in elementary school. One with an uncommonly good mind for mathematics. He would have taken me from my sad trailer-park life. He would have turned me into... what? A monster? A whore?

I never found out because Damon sacrificed himself for me.

Does that excuse him for turning into a monster?

For turning into a whore?

He leads me up the stairs to the room I know

is his bedroom. The room where he once cradled me in his arms after his father attacked me. Are there more half-naked people in that large bed? Are they dancing and having sex like the ones downstairs?

The closed wooden door doesn't provide any hints to what's inside.

Damon turns the latch. The silence is almost tangible, a wild relief after the chaos below. I suck in a deep breath from even the nearness to it—to calm and quiet.

He nods his head, a small gesture of chivalry at odds with the party downstairs.

I step into the room, dragging my little suitcase behind me. It suddenly feels unbearably intimate—the secondhand luggage with my clothes inside. My panties and my little bottles of shampoo that I took out in the airport security line. All of that in Damon Scott's bedroom, as if I plan to stay with him. As if we're lovers.

"The chances of being found reduce at an exponential rate every day in the case of missing persons."

My words ring in the air, testament to my lack of social graces. Other women can swing their hips and smile in that seductive way. Other women are downstairs.

Damon leans against the wall, looking unmoved by my words. "What makes you think she's missing?"

I blink. "Because she's gone. She's not in her apartment. Not on campus."

"I mean, what makes you think she left against her will? Were there signs of a struggle? A note written in blood? What makes you think she didn't leave on her own?"

I'm standing near the door, unable to move closer. Unable to leave. "Why would she do that?"

"Why wouldn't she?" he counters, as casual as if we're debating whether it will rain today. *The clouds are heavy. They might pass through.* "Maybe everything wasn't perfect with Gabriel Miller."

Goose bumps rise on my skin, because everything wasn't perfect. She was worried about Gabriel, worried and too afraid to tell him. *I can't help but think one of these days he's going to go away and not come back.* Instead she was the one who went away.

"Why wouldn't Gabriel tell you about her?"

"You'd have to ask him."

"I'm asking *you.* I thought you were friends." Gabriel had been here, in the Den, the day that Damon brought my wet and shivering body here. The day he'd brought me back to life.

Damon unfolds himself from the wall, standing taller than he did even five minutes ago. This
man commands more than a room. He could
move an army. And he approaches me like I'm his
enemy. "Darling," he says softly. "I let you leave
this city. I let you leave *me*."

His desire is electric, a live current through
my whole body, from my core spreading out to
my fingertips. "You had nothing to do with it."

He ignores that. "And now here you are with
your Bambi eyes, acting like you didn't just walk
into the dark fucking forest. What am I supposed
to do with you?"

I swallow. "You could help me find Avery."

A small smile. "I thought you wanted me to
find your father."

"Can't we do both?"

"Maybe. Maybe not. What if you could only
pick one, baby genius? What's the calculation you
use to weigh a human life? Did they teach you
that in college?"

There's lead in my stomach, a heavy weight
full of worry and guilt. And a terrible fear that I'm
somehow the cause of this. "It's been seven days.
That's how long Avery's been gone."

"And?"

"She's your sister. Don't you care what happens to her?"

"Ah, dear old dad. I'm not sure that his infidelity constitutes a family."

I stare at him, shocked. "He was married to your mother?"

Jonathan Scott has always seemed more legend than man. I can't imagine him doing something as mundane as getting married. Who could convince him to say vows? Who would want to?

"How do you know she didn't leave on her own?" he asks softly.

My lips press together. I know it deep in my bones, which ignores everything I believe about numbers and symbols. This is some other kind of knowledge.

"In fact," he says, using a low version of that showman's voice. "That puts those terrible statistics in a different light, doesn't it? Realizing that some of the women that go missing do it on purpose. They do it to escape. And they don't want to be found."

"Avery didn't do that."

He speaks in slow challenge. "How do you know?"

"Because I was there," I burst out, my voice shaking. "I was sleeping when she disappeared.

Right next to her. She asked me to spend the night because she was afraid, and I failed her."

Tears prick my eyes, and I turn away from him—from the warm yellow glow of the lamp, from the tall silhouette of a man who doesn't want my grief. He doesn't care about it. It's an inconvenience to him, and even that's my fault. Who would he be if he'd escaped instead of me?

Damon Scott is too sharp, too strong. Too real in every way.

I didn't cry when Avery went missing, not when the police came and took my statement. Not when they escorted me to the station and made me wait in an interrogation room for three hours. Not even when Gabriel Miller arrived and looked at me with cold calculation, as if he was figuring out whether I had hurt Avery or had a hand in it. He must have decided against it, because I'm still alive.

Damon destroys the walls I've kept around myself for years. Rips through the dreamlike state I've been in since I found myself alone in Avery's bed, wishing every second to wake up. I'm awake now, but she's still gone. There's a piercing ache in my chest with no numbers to shield me.

The air shifts. I don't hear him move, but he doesn't have to make a sound. He could leave me here, the scared little girl unworthy of his time. He could find one of the beautiful women downstairs. I already know they would do anything for him, when I can barely bring myself to breathe.

Something appears in front of me. He's holding out a sheet of paper. I blink to clear my vision. A single tear drops onto the page, leaving a large gray dot. There's ink scribbled here.

Two rows of jumbled letters. A row of random numbers.

"What is this?" I say, my voice thick with grief and confusion.

"You tell me, baby genius. It arrived seven days ago. The same day Avery James disappeared."

Chapter Eleven

"**W**HAT IS IT?" I ask even though I already know. It's a puzzle, and there's a part of me that yearned for this. For a puzzle I can't immediately solve. One without a textbook to explain it to me. I've been searching my whole life for something I can't unscramble, for a riddle without an answer.

Which makes me feel like a terrible person.

"Maybe nothing. Gibberish. Or a message from Avery herself."

"Or a ransom note."

"Why would a kidnapper put his ransom note in code? Doesn't he want to get paid?"

Okay, that's a good point. But this is still the best lead to where Avery has gone. The only one. "You think it's related or you wouldn't have shown me."

"I told you to leave."

"And you didn't throw this away when it came."

"I have no interest in games." His words are punctuated by a crash from downstairs.

The thought of that beautiful foyer chandelier broken on the marble entry makes me wince. "Not interested in games? Then what do you call what's happening downstairs?"

"Boredom," he says.

I know my expression reflects my doubt at that. There was a full harem of beautiful women down there. Men, too. Does he sleep with both of them? "Aren't you worried about what they're breaking?"

A dark look. "Does it matter?"

"Yes," I say even though the admission feels too personal. The Den may be a bed of crime and masculine power, but it's also the only place I felt truly safe.

He studies me as if he can see under my skin, beneath the college student and even the mathematician, all the way to the scared little girl who's never trusted anyone but him.

With a short nod he turns away and pulls out a shiny black phone. He murmurs something I can't make out, slipping it back into his pocket a moment later. He stares at me with those dark, fathomless eyes.

One, two, three seconds later. The beat stops.

Silence rings in my ears. My bones feel unnaturally still without the heavy bass.

"What happened?" I ask faintly.

"I told them to leave." He says it plainly, without guilt or grandeur. It's in that matter-of-fact tone that he admits how much my words matter. How much *I* matter. All I had to do is say that I didn't want them breaking his things, and they stop.

"Does everyone listen to what you say?"

"Usually," he says, his expression wry. "You're an exception to the rule."

It's too unnerving, the way he looks at me. Taking me apart, uncovering every secret with methodical determination. That's supposed to be my job. It would be better if he yelled at me. This subtle understanding is too much to take. "I'll call Gabriel. Tell him about the message."

"No."

I pause, my hand halfway to my back pocket where my phone sits. "What?"

"What's the point of telling him? He has no chance of figuring it out. Not until you do."

The paper burns my fingers, everything it represents—both about Avery and about me. "This isn't my area of study. Ciphers. Encryption. We should find someone else."

"Is there anyone else you would trust with Avery's life?"

Somehow I know the message is meant for me. Did Avery send this? Did she know that I would go to Damon Scott? We talked about him the night she disappeared. Could she have sent this to him knowing it would find its way to me?

And why bother putting it into code? She could have written *Dear Penny* at the top of a regular note. For that matter she could have scribbled something on paper when she left the hotel room.

"He has a right to know," I say slowly. "He loves her. If she sent this—"

"*If* she sent this. We don't know. What's the point of getting his hopes up when it might be unrelated? Furthermore, she sent this to me. What if she didn't want him to see it?"

My stomach clenches, because there are too many unknowns. "I don't know what to do."

A look of sympathy passes over Damon's handsome face. "Did I give you the impression you had a choice? My apologies. You don't need to worry. There's nothing for you to decide."

The certainty in his voice is a cold finger along my spine. "What does that mean?"

"It means you'll be staying here until you

solve this."

It's almost a relief, the pain. The end I've been waiting for. Waking up after a beautiful dream. "No."

There's a catch in my voice proving I don't mean it. He smiles a little. "You can fight if it makes you feel better. I'll enjoy pinning you down."

And I realize how sometimes you end up in a web. Not through traps and trickery, but walking right through the front door. "So why don't you?"

"I don't have to. You want to stay. You need to know what that message means. And what's more, you'll get off on figuring it out. We'll both enjoy this."

"I won't," I say through clenched teeth.

A low laugh fills the large room. "I suppose we'll have to wait and find out."

The bed looms between us, once an innocuous piece of furniture, now a weapon. A wall. "I'm not sleeping in this bed with you."

"Of course not," he says, gesturing to a side door. "You'll be in there."

It's too much to hope that there's a hallway. A small little guest room with a lock I can turn on the doorknob. My feet are filled with lead as I find out.

The doorknob turns easily, revealing a very dark room. It takes me a moment to figure out what I'm looking at—not a closet. Almost as small, though. There's a bed so thin and flat it must be a cot. And a chest of drawers. The furniture here is solid but plain, in contrast to the ornate carvings and heavy brocade in Damon's bedroom. No other door leading out, only this one, leading in.

Beside the bed is a small bell attached to the wall. I stare at it, puzzled. And then turn to look over my shoulder. Beside Damon's overlarge bed, there's an old-fashioned switch.

My stomach drops as I realize what this is. Servant's quarters.

Made for someone who serves the king.

CHAPTER TWELVE

I SPEND THE evening working at the plain desk, a stack of empty paper beside me where I can try out various ciphers. The Caeser cipher is a basic substitution of alphabet letters, really only child's play. One displacement makes *B* mean *A* and *C* mean *B*. Two displacements, three. There are twenty-five distinct ciphers, assuming both sets of alphabets go in the proper order.

If the letters are jumbled, there are over 400 trillion permutations to try. And that doesn't even get into homophonic substitutions. Or the infinite number of other forms of codes.

The only thing I know for sure is that we're in big trouble.

It's like trying to crack a modern-day bank safe with a hammer and a pick. It's technically possible but only if you have eternity. That's how Dr. Stanhope has taught me to think—in abstract absolutes.

Meanwhile there are two lines of text that

have a very real application.

I'm used to late nights with my head bent over my paper, but my neck aches by the time I turn off the light and climb into the cot. It's surprisingly comfortable for what amounts to a pad of cotton—or maybe I'm too exhausted to care. It seems like a hundred years ago that I stepped into a cab at the Emerald's staff driveway to head to the airport.

My view isn't so different from the one there. A small rectangular ceiling on top of a small rectangular room. That's how I justify my decision to stay. I couldn't go back to Daddy's apartment, not with the lock busted. And I don't have money to blow on even a cheap motel.

That reasoning worked for me when I sat down to work, more focused on the code than my sleeping arrangements. It feels a little more sinister as I look at the door that leads to Damon's bedroom—the only way out of here.

He was a gentleman when I used the bathroom to change into a loose T-shirt and sweatpants. When I brushed my teeth. How long will that last? What if I have to get up in the middle of the night?

There's plenty of room in the bed with him. Would I have felt safer if he expected me to sleep beside him? No, I wouldn't. *But I would have felt more like his equal.*

With this move he's making it clear that I'm not.

The small silver dome of the bell barely glints in the darkness. What if he rings the bell? Am I supposed to answer it? I definitely couldn't sleep through it if he tried. And what would he ask me to do? To get him a cup of water? What did rich people need at night that they can't do themselves?

My cheeks heat as I think of a darker purpose for that bell.

He might want a different kind of service.

I won't do that. I won't. But I can't deny the way my body responds to the idea. It always seems to get warm when he's around, my skin flushed, my clothes suddenly chafing.

That's how I fall asleep, imagining the bell ringing, thinking of Damon's heavy-lidded look, pretending that he wants me for something more than solving a puzzle.

I push out onto a rough-water dreamland, every wave a dark reminder of what's underneath the surface. Memories mix with a dangerous future, until I'm not sure what really happened.

I'm back in our old apartment, the one I share

with Mama and whoever she's seeing at the time. My small clock with the kitty whiskers says it's morning, but my head is pounding. It's hard for me to sleep over the music she plays. I push the sheets off my legs and cross the carpet.

Her bedroom door is open, her sheets rumpled and empty. I want to check for her in the kitchen. Sometimes she makes French toast, if she's feeling good. I hope there's French toast.

I start to walk that way, but the bathroom light is on, the door cracked open.

And there's a weird smell in the air. Not the sweet stuff she smokes or the heavy scent of alcohol. This is something metal, like the way my hands smell after going across the monkey bars.

My heart pounds as I take a step closer.

Close enough to push the door open…

I sit up in bed, gasping. Only a dream. Another dream just like all the others. And it always ends before I see Mama in the bathtub, floating in a pool of pink water, eyes open and still. It's a blessing that it stops before then, but also a curse. I can't move past what I can't even see.

My bladder is heavy, which means I'll have to find a bathroom, sooner rather than later.

There are only a few seconds of deliberation— what if he's out there? What if he's not? The body doesn't have much patience. It could be two hours since I turned off the lamp—or twenty. There are no windows, not even a small one like in my room at the Emerald. My room there overlooks the delivery alley, the steady stream of bakers and farmers and laundry trucks a comfort I don't have now.

I push open the door to a room that's quiet… except for a faint snore.

It's almost sweet, that snore. It makes him seem more human.

The room is too dark to see him clearly, but I can tell he's in the bed. Light frames the curtains, saying we've reached tomorrow already. I use the bathroom and brush my teeth, things that might seem mundane if I didn't see Damon Scott's razor right beside the sink. Completely ordinary if I weren't in a bathroom made of marble—white stone with large cool pieces and deep gold striations.

When I step back into the dark bedroom, I know that I should go back to my little closet-room. I should sit down at the desk and keep working on the code. Or maybe I should walk out the door, escape while I can. Am I a prisoner? He's asleep right now, his large body still on the much larger bed. Now would be the time to leave.

I have the code memorized. That happened approximately two seconds after seeing the paper. I could continue to work on it from a motel I can't really afford.

Instead I find myself taking a step closer to the bed. Watching the shadows until I catch the rhythm of his breathing—and realize I'm looking at muscled abs on a naked torso. God.

As my eyes adjust, I confirm he's not wearing his shirt, his broad chest and strong arms bare. Dark lashes rest against his cheeks, which seems to conceal him more than a three-piece suit ever could. My gaze drifts lower, to where the sheet doesn't quite reach his hips.

He's not wearing anything at all.

My cheeks turn hot with the realization. He's naked right now.

"Like what you see?" he says, his voice startling in the dark.

I shiver, darting my gaze to meet his. "No."

It's an instinctive denial—more to being caught than what he looks like. *No, I wasn't*— His low laugh rushes along the darkness, raising goose bumps on my arms. He doesn't look offended. He looks challenged, which is so much worse. "Come here."

"No," I repeat, but this time there's a tremor

in my voice.

"Be a good little servant girl," he says, his voice low.

The word shivers through me, a tactile vibration. *Servant girl.* It's like he found my deepest fear, an ancient emotional bruise, and pressed on it—and perversely, so perversely, it feels good.

"That's who the room is for," he says. "But I'm sure you figured that out. You've always been too clever. Too fucking clever, and look where it gets you. Nowhere."

I shudder. "I'm not touching you."

He throws his head back in a laugh so reckless, so pure I'm almost jealous. What must it feel like, to be that carefree, that confident? "I haven't gotten to that part yet. You're reading ahead."

"I'm not having sex with you, either."

"Come here."

I take a step closer, hating myself, fearing myself. Who is this creature who obeys Damon Scott? I'm afraid of him—not what he'll make me do, but that he'll make me like it.

"A little closer," he says, coaxing. "I'm not going to hurt you. Or would you like that?"

Somehow I'm at the end of the bed, the fronts of my thighs pressed against the thick mattress. I've given up all the space between us, all the distance. But I won't give in without a fight. "Maybe you'd like that. Maybe it runs in the family."

He doesn't flinch, but I feel his recoil in the air. "Is that what you think?"

He'd rip my heart to shreds with that half smile on his handsome face. He would destroy any chance I ever had for a normal life with a regal incline of his head. He was right to put me in that little servant room. That's all the power I have here. Anything else is only a dream.

"You know what? There were a hundred beautiful women here last night. Summon one of them to your bed if you need entertainment. Because it won't be me."

CHAPTER THIRTEEN

I T'S A RELIEF that he lets me work the rest of the morning, my hands and mind plying furiously on the puzzle at hand. A relief that I can immerse myself in a land of numbers—free from pain and worry and guilt. A knock comes at midday. My heart thuds double-time as I stare at the plain white door.

A tray sits just outside my small room, no one in sight. Did Damon bring this to me? That would make him the servant, not me. No, it must have been someone who works for him. Someone who prepared this roast beef sandwich and fresh potato salad.

Someone who prepared my tea sweet, exactly how I like it.

Instead of eating, I step into the upstairs hallway, listening for footsteps. None.

Only when I'm halfway down the wide staircase can I hear voices. One male. One female. Maybe he did call one of the women from last night. My chest burns with unbidden jealousy. So what if he has sex with someone else? He could have sex with a million women—and he probably has.

"She's my sister," a low voice says. Damon. "I have a right to know."

"And you're being informed."

"Days after she's gone."

The woman seems unafraid of his low tone. "We all know you only found out about the sibling relationship recently. And you weren't exactly close."

"We might have been closer if Gabriel didn't tell her terrible things about me."

"Are you saying he lied?"

"Of course not," Damon says, his voice light. "I'm a monster. An animal with sharp claws and no cage whatsoever. Isn't that right, Penny?"

I startle in the shadows of the lower step, ashamed that he caught me listening. In two steps I'm standing in the dining room, where Damon faces off with a beautiful young woman in a business suit. Her dark hair falls straight past her shoulders. Her ebony eyes glitter with challenge.

Two cups of coffee are between them, the scent potent.

Whether they're weapons or shields, I'm not

sure.

"He's worried about her," I say because it's true. They can argue about whether Damon Scott is a good man or a bad man, but I know he cares what happens to Avery.

The woman doesn't turn her head when she addresses me. "Pack your things."

"She's not going anywhere," Damon says.

"We have reason to believe she's being held against her will."

Damon barks a laugh. "A spy? How much does Gabriel pay him to take it up the ass?"

Someone here last night reported to Gabriel? Is that why this woman came—to rescue me? If she's the white knight, that casts Damon Scott as the dragon. An appropriate metaphor considering he looks ready to breathe fire. It occurs to me that the more he laughs, the more furious he is.

"I don't want to leave," I say quickly, trying to avert disaster.

"Don't be afraid," the woman says, sounding imperious. "He can't touch you."

Damon's dark eyes flash. "I can do whatever I want to her, but that's nothing compared to what I'll do to someone who tries to take her away from me. That includes you, Nina."

Nina opens her mouth to say something, but I

beat her to it. "I said I don't want to leave. This is my life, and I make the decisions for me. I'm not going anywhere until Avery is found. I'm not going anywhere until I solve the cipher."

A clink of silver on china as Nina drops her spoon into the cup.

Too late I realize she doesn't know about the code.

Sometimes I pretend that people walk around with numbers flashing above their heads—the number of words they say a minute, the amount of money they make a month. The percentage of time they lie when they open their mouths. It helps me get through the world, surrounded by unknowns.

The number above Damon Scott's head is a four, the place where all numbers converge. He gives a resigned sigh. "There was a note sent to me the night Avery disappeared."

Nina sucks in a breath. "Why didn't you tell us?"

"How would I have known?" he asks, his voice lethal in its softness. "I had no idea what it was about until Penny showed up last night. Even now I'm not certain it's related."

"Let me see it," she says.

He looks ready to refuse, but I'm not going to

hold back something that could help Avery. "I'll show it to you, and what I've tried so far."

Damon stands with Nina in old-world courtesy, but he makes no move to follow us upstairs. I hesitate, uncertain whether I should let someone invade his space—especially without him being present.

He gives me a wry smile. "Go on upstairs. Show her whatever you want, Penny. But when she leaves, she leaves the note here. She leaves you, too."

Chapter Fourteen

NINA STUDIES MY work with a sharp eye. Her questions are smart and methodical. "Do you have a background in mathematics?" I ask, almost too eager to find a colleague.

"Computer science," she says. "We need to get this plugged into some decryption algorithms as soon as possible. A brute force attack by hand would take forever."

"That's a good idea," I say, and I mean that.

Nina's eyebrows rise. "But?"

"No, I mean it *is* a good idea." Sometimes people write their computer passwords on paper. It could be a lot of different electronic things. But I have a feeling it isn't. A feeling isn't logic. It isn't anything I can verify or back up, but it's there nonetheless. "The medium. It could be part of the message."

"Telling us what?"

"How to decode it," I say, unable to say more. Strangely unwilling.

"Is this her handwriting?" she asks, sounding dubious.

"I'm not sure," I admit. "Is Gabriel still at the Emerald? We can ask for a sample."

"We can do a lot more than that. We can get a handwriting expert. He has a lot of resources, and he's willing to use every last one to find her." She reaches for the note, and I pull it back in time. "It will help to have the original."

"Not if you're going to plug the numbers into a computer. Handwriting analysis can work off the picture, too."

She smiles. "Are you on Damon's side?"

"I'm on whatever side gets Avery back safely," I say in total honesty.

Her expression reveals nothing. She would be brilliant at poker, if she played. And that's exactly what she's doing—playing a game, this one with far higher stakes than clay chips on green velvet. "Are you in Damon's bed?"

Nina hadn't blinked when I showed her into Damon's bedroom—or when I continued into the small closet-room where we're standing now. She had eyes only for the cipher.

I wave a hand, a little relieved that the sleeping arrangements are apparent. Mostly embarrassed that this is where he put me. "I have my own bed."

"That doesn't mean you won't join him."

My cheeks heat, memories of Damon's strong body flush in my mind. From the outside he seems lean, but without the cover of his suit I could see ropes of muscle and layers of scars that speak to merciless strength. I could see the endless lines of ink etched into him. Monsters with only one eye. A wild woman with snakes for hair. And waves for miles of muscle.

"I won't."

A smile curves her lips, making her look like a dark-skinned Mona Lisa. "I wouldn't judge you. There are plenty of women who've wanted him over the years. Plenty who've tried to get where you are."

My tongue feels thick. "In a servant's room?"

"Any way they can get him, I suppose. If you're into that kind of thing."

I blink, uncertain whether she's talking about the man or the servitude. "What kind of thing?"

"Ownership."

The line between me and my composure is made of steel, a long taut string. It snaps with an almost audible creak. I lean back in the small wooden chair, whiplash making it hard to speak. "He doesn't own me."

"Right," she says, turning back to the cipher. "I'll take high-resolution pictures of the code, plus your work—if you don't mind."

"It's fine," I manage. "If it will help."

I set the note down directly under the lamp, studying the random assortment of letters and numbers along with her. Something about the sight of them stirs a memory, but I can't bring it to the surface.

Nina uses her phone to take multiple pictures of the note, making sure each one uploads completely. Then she snaps quicker images of my work product—mostly my handwriting scribbled down with intermittent question marks.

"Gabriel's going to find her," I say, trying to convince myself more than her.

"Of course he is," she says, a little sadly, and I realize that she means dead or alive.

She turns to leave and pauses at the door. "You know, before? I didn't only mean that he would own you. It could be that he's been waiting for someone strong enough to own him."

My laugh bursts out of me, a strange relief after the pressure of the last week. "No way."

Her smile is indulgent. "Are you sure?"

"He definitely thinks he owns me." Because he bought me. He *won* me, but that's not something I'm going to explain to her. If she works for Gabriel Miller, then she might already know. It's strange to talk about something so personal with a stranger, but in some ways that's the only kind of person I could share this with. It would be too humiliating to dissect with someone I know. "Look where he put me. I can't even leave my room without going through him."

Which puts a much more sinister slant on my stay here. I insisted that I wanted to stay before, and it's true. What happens when I want to leave? Will he let me?

"Yes, but look at the way he protects you."

My eyebrows lower, because I hadn't realized I was in danger. "What do you mean?"

She looks at my little bed, the plain desk. "This room. It doesn't only keep you inside. It keeps everyone else out. They'd have to go through him to get to you."

I swallow hard, realizing that she's telling the truth. It's a place of both shame and honor. Which one did Damon Scott intend? Maybe both, because he's nothing if not perverse.

It's been strange not having the nightmares, as if Damon's presence outside my room keeps them away. I feel almost guilty about that, as if I should be more messed up over Avery's disappearance.

Like I should have terrible dreams every night. I've put my whole life on hold looking for her, but it doesn't feel like enough. I'm not sure anything would.

"No one's trying to get to me," I say, but it comes out as a question.

"Right," she says. "The Den is the safest place in the city. And this room is the safest place inside."

The words are meant to be reassuring, but a small seedling of uncertainty plants itself in my stomach. The safest place. I repeat the words, wondering why I don't find comfort. Maybe because the safer I need to be, the more I'm afraid of the invisible threats that made it this way.

CHAPTER FIFTEEN

A GROWL BREAKS through the silence, making me startle in bed. My gaze flies to the silver bell on the bed, but it's still and silent. The hair on the back of my neck rises.

It fills the air, a sense of dread. The sound of an animal in pain.

I step out of bed and open the door, only one centimeter. Only enough to see the shadowed expanse of bed, the large figure writhing on it. It strikes me then, that I haven't had a nightmare since I first slept in this room. It's someone else's nightmare now. I should pretend I don't hear. I think that's what he would want me to do, but I can't leave him like this.

Flashes of bare skin and dark ink. Muscles straining.

A growl low enough to rumble beneath my feet.

"Damon?"

Self-assured. Smooth. That's how Damon

Scott looks every other second, wearing his three-piece suits and that devastating smile. Even yesterday morning, his muscled body reclining in bed, he was the epitome of strength and masculinity.

Only now he's covered in a sheen of sweat, ropes of scar tissue standing in stark relief to his flushed skin. He throws his head back on the pillow, his mouth in a grimace, teeth glinting.

He looks like a wild animal. He *sounds* like one, both menacing and afraid at once.

I'm trembling as I move a step closer. It doesn't take a genius to figure out he's dangerous like this, dangerous *always,* but his pain calls to me. It's too much like my own.

I reach for him in the dark.

His skin feels clammy. Muscles twitch beneath my touch.

He moves in a blur of flesh and fury. A hard pull on my wrist. A heavy weight on my body. The bed is somehow at my back. I'm staring up into eyes so black they seem limitless. The city sky without a single star in sight. His lips are pulled back, chest heaving.

The bar of his arm presses against my throat.

I suck in a breath, but there's not much room. Panic clenches around my stomach, making it hard to breathe. Between his body bearing down on me and his forearm on my windpipe, I don't have very long. Dark spots dance in front of my eyes. Struggle burns through me, desperate, desolate.

"Please," I whisper, my lips strangely swollen.

His eyes focus on me. They widen in shock.

The next instant he's off me, standing five feet away from the bed. I gasp in ragged breaths. The air is sharper now, sweeter. I kneel on the bed, panting and shaking.

"What the fuck?" he says, low, his voice raw.

"You were—" I draw in another fortifying breath. "You were having a nightmare."

He looks incredulous. "I could have killed you."

"I'm sorry," I say, but that's a lie.

I'm sorry he's going through this alone. I'm sorry he feels guilty for pinning me down. I'm sorry for a lot of things in my life, but not waking him from a nightmare.

He gives a hollow laugh, devoid of humor. "Christ."

My lungs don't seem to work correctly anymore. They can't bring in enough air. Can't push the air all the way out. It's too hard to form words. I can only look at him, pleading with my eyes.

Then he's by my side, rubbing my back in gentle circles, holding me with a tenderness I wouldn't have thought possible. "Breathe, baby. Breathe. I've got you. I've got you for as long as it takes."

Empty nothings. That's what Mama used to say about words like that. They were just things people say without meaning them, but they don't feel like nothing. They feel like everything.

I've got you for as long as it takes.

My breath slows down, evens out. And true to his word, Damon doesn't leave my side. A final shot of panic eases out of me.

And just like that I become aware that Damon is naked. That he's naked and *touching* me.

My gaze snaps away from him, but it's too late. I saw the column of his cock against his thigh. I saw the darker tip. Is it always that big? My cheeks burn hot. Even without looking at him, his cock is all I can see. It's emblazoned in my mind, dark and hard and intimidating.

His hand on my back stills. The circles were comforting. Maybe even fatherly.

When his hand rests against my upper back, there's nothing fatherly about it. There's warmth and tension. A beautiful tautness that promises so much more than this.

My breath catches.

"Don't do that," he says.

"What?"

"Don't want me."

Is that what this strange feeling is, like my arteries and veins are tied into knots, my body feverish? Is this desire? I don't even have to wonder how he knows what I'm feeling. He always seems to know, like it's written on my skin. Words like *naive* and *hopeless*. Words like *virgin*.

"I should go," I whisper without moving.

I think if he took his hand off my back, I could have left. If he'd been the one to break contact. Instead he sat there, the warm press of his large hand a conduit for this strange electricity between us.

Dr. Stanhope had held me, and I felt warm and tingly.

It felt *good*.

Damon's hand on my back doesn't feel good. It feels like a warning and a prayer. It feels like a thousand volts of lust. There's no breaking this connection. I can't imagine wanting to.

And this is only one-sided, energy flowing from him to me.

I don't know where to touch him or whether I should. Somehow my hand lifts, all on its own. The back of my hand brushes his arm. It's the completion of the circuit, and it sends a surge of sensation through me strong enough to be pain. There's no time to dwell on that, because Damon uses the momentum to drag me closer. I fall into him, his body catching mine. It's too dark to see anything but the gloss of dark eyes, the flash of white teeth. The sparks behind my eyelids as his hand cups my cheek.

His breath touches my lips, a soft exhale that might have been a word.

Then his mouth closes over mine. A kiss, but that isn't the right word. A claiming. A question. An unbearable relief after long years of drought. He drinks me down, taking more than he has a right to, but I learn something—that I have more to give.

A moan escapes me. My whole body leans toward him, wanting more, wanting to *give* him more. He takes it with greedy presumption, the king accepting his right. And me eager to serve.

"Penny," he murmurs. "Sweet Penny."

He slides his hand behind my neck, tilting my head back. His tongue nudges my mouth open. It's a firm demand, one that I'm helpless against.

Open. Vulnerable. A stroke against my tongue, that's my reward. Merciless intimacy so raw it makes my chest ache.

I make a sound—frightened.

It seems to wake him up from some wild slumber. He pushes back from me, making the whole bed rock. *Slam* as the solid wood bed frame hits the wall. "Christ," he mutters.

The reprieve bites into me like a cold wind, whistling and desolate. "Wait."

"Get back to your room," he says, his voice sharp.

Sometimes strength means standing up to your enemies. Sometimes it means standing *with* them. "I don't want to go."

His hand on my wrist feels completely different than before. Not comforting. Not electric. This is something else. *Menacing.* He leans over me, making my heart pound in solemn warning. "I'll fuck you if you want me to, honey. And then push you out of my bed."

There are castles inside me, built on hopes I didn't know I had. Not until they crumble. His words ring with truth. That's what he'd do to me, and God, what else did I expect?

He presses close enough to brush his lips against my cheek, a perverse sweetness. "What'll it be, Penny? Are you going to spread your legs for me?"

"You're a bastard," I say between clenched teeth.

He pushes me away with a rough laugh. "Guilty as charged."

It's not him I'm mad at when I stand on the cold wood floor in my pajamas. It's the man who made him this way. Maybe he would have been an asshole no matter who his father was. But Jonathan Scott has left his mark on this man in more ways than one.

Even the darkness can't completely hide the scars on Damon's body.

"What was your dream about?" I ask softly.

His cocky amusement fades away. "I think you know."

Jonathan Scott is a spider in the city of Tanglewood, spinning webs that can catch any one of us. It caught me once. I remember dark green tiles, black soil. Water rising. "He only had me one night."

"One night was too fucking long."

And how many nights did a small boy have to endure?

How many nights did a child suffer at the hands of a monster?

How many nights does Damon Scott suffer his nightmares by himself? "No one should have to go through the nightmares alone. If you want to kiss me... or if you want to hurt me... you know where to find me."

CHAPTER SIXTEEN

DAMON DOESN'T COME see me the rest of the night, which isn't a surprise. The shock on his face had been gratifying, but it doesn't change anything. He doesn't want me.

Or he doesn't *want* to want me, which almost feels worse.

Unable to sleep I go to work on the code and make a breakthrough.

My stomach sinks when I realize I'm looking at a complex polynomial curve. I feel sick, not because I can't solve it but because it proves the message wasn't sent by Avery. And that it was probably sent for me. The letters convert via hex code, which is simple enough, but the polynomial curve they describe is much more advanced. Graduate level math. Who would know how to make this? Who would know that I could solve it?

The code translates into two words: *COME ALONE*.

It feels much more sinister now, and my

throat clenches as I imagine all the horrible things that could be happening to her. It feels wrong to have a bed—even a small cot—when she might be in danger. Wrong to eat when she might be hungry.

Should I wake up Damon? Except he already sent me away.

And besides, the code isn't completely solved. There's still a bottom row of numbers that could mean anything. A signature? A location?

COME ALONE isn't something we can act on.

Come where?

I fall into a restless sleep and wake up when faint light seeps under the door.

When I step outside, I find an empty bedroom and a tray of breakfast. French toast made from thick brioche bread, fresh cut berries, a small carafe of coffee. This must be what it's like for Avery to have room service delivered, I think with a flash of envy. And then immediately shiver with guilt.

Wherever she is now, she probably doesn't have room service. Every bite of the delicious breakfast fills me with both illicit comfort and terrible dread.

I take the empty tray downstairs, half expecting to find Damon lurking in the corner or an army of maids and cooks at his service. It's eerily quiet, almost like I'm walking through a museum.

In the kitchen there's a woman reading a magazine.

She's wearing a black T-shirt and blazer with jeans, her dark hair pulled into a strict ponytail. She looks up and smiles at me. "Good morning."

"Good morning," I say, a little wary. She's beautiful enough to have been one of the women dancing in bikini tops and leather skirts that first night, but I wouldn't recognize her if she was. Not with my memories of that night hazy, lights flashing, smoke in the air.

Not with her face scrubbed clean of any makeup.

I put the tray down on the counter beside an empty sink, wondering if I should do the dishes.

"Do you need anything?" she asks, her tone neutral.

It feels strange that I don't know whether she's Damon's guest or servant. Then again it's strange that I don't know that about myself. "I'm sorry, who are you?"

She gives a tinkling laugh. "My name's Hiro-mi, but you can call me Hiro. I'm your personal security."

Personal security. Does that mean she's keeping

me in the house or defending me from what's outside? With Damon it's probably both, the same way he uses the small room to possess me and protect me.

I sit down across the high kitchen tabletop. "Well, hi."

"Hi," she says back, as if nothing could disturb that calm composure. Probably nothing can.

"So you work for Damon?"

She nods. "I've done a few jobs for him, but this is the first time I've provided bodyguard services."

"You weren't by chance the person who made that French toast for breakfast?"

"My version of cooking is peanut butter on toast."

Who made the tray for me then? "So what other jobs have you done for Damon?"

"You would have to ask him."

Her answer doesn't surprise me, but I have to try. This is one of the few people I've had access to who knows Damon outside of my father and Avery. "Are you the only guard here?"

"The only one inside the house."

"Isn't it kind of a big property to have only one person?" The security procedures at the Emerald had been akin to an airport, probably tighter. Armed guards on rotating patrol. Background checks. Security cameras. All the things Gabriel Miller had done to keep Avery safe, but it didn't work.

"I think Damon Scott has the best security system there is," Hiro says. "Reputation."

No one would dare attack the Den, except the one person I fear the most. His father. But Jonathan Scott is long dead. My last memory is of him strung up, being tortured, Gabriel and Damon's joint retribution for the man's misdeeds.

A shiver runs through me. "Do you know where Damon is?"

"Yes."

She doesn't offer anything more than that, and it makes me smile a little. "Okay."

"If you need to get in touch with him, I can call."

The memory of last night's kiss is too fresh in my mind. "No, thank you. But do you mind if I just... talk to you a little more? I know that probably isn't in your job description, but it's a little isolating upstairs."

Her expression softens. "Of course not. I get so used to working alone, but there are times it's hard."

I glance at the glossy page of the magazine

that I can't quite read. "I guess you have a lot of time to pass. Then again I guess boring is a good thing in your line of work."

"This is related to work." She flips the magazine back to its cover, revealing the stark letters *GUN DIGEST*. Something silver and terrifying is pictured on the front.

My eyes widen. "Wow."

"Well, not only work," she says with a private smile. "We all have our hobbies."

We all have our addictions. Drugs. Gambling. My addiction is something maybe more dangerous. Someone with a wicked smile. "I understand."

"And the truth is, I prefer action. I don't usually accept jobs like this, but Damon Scott can be very persuasive when he wants something."

My stomach twists in jealousy, even though I have no hold on him. *No right to him, actually.* "Why did he want you to take the job so bad?"

"Aside from the fact that I'm the best?" she asks without arrogance. "Because I'm a woman, probably. And I'm guarding the woman he's keeping in his bedroom."

My mind trips on the implication, that Damon Scott might be jealous. "It's not like that between us."

"Maybe not, but it wouldn't matter. If I wanted to steal you away from him, I could."

I laugh out loud, a flood of relief to find normalcy in such a strange situation. She laughs with me, even though I'm pretty sure she's dead serious.

"So what kind of information does a gun magazine have. New guns?"

"New models. New attachments. Firsthand accounts of combat, that kind of thing."

"That sounds..." *Terrifying.* "Specific to your profession. Is there a wide gun enthusiast audience?"

"Wider than you probably want to think about," she answers almost cheerfully. "But you don't have to worry. As long as I'm here, you're safe. Though you should probably stay away from the windows."

I blink at her, thinking of the small room I have upstairs with no windows. Thinking of Nina's words about it. *This room. It doesn't only keep you inside. It keeps everyone else out. They'd have to go through him to get to you.*

CHAPTER SEVENTEEN

I WAIT UNTIL midafternoon before venturing out again. Outside the room there's a landing with a wide balcony and curving stairs. I follow the scent of roasting chicken, my mouth watering in anticipation. Whatever dish is being prepared in the kitchen, it will probably end up on a beautiful tray outside my door.

Who's cooking it? And why have I never met that person?

Maybe it's not an important mystery in context, but it pulls me in.

As I get closer to the kitchen I hear strains of classical music coming from the speakers perched in the corner of the dining room. It's soft enough that I can still hear a faint clatter of metal pots inside.

I push open the swinging door, struck silent by what I see.

Damon Scott, his white shirt sleeves rolled up, his jacket and vest draped over a barstool, stirring something as it simmers on a professional stainless steel cooktop. Proof is tucked into every corner— the fresh parsley chopped on a board, a home- made broth defrosting on the counter.

"What are you doing?" I ask, proving how very little IQ points actually count for anything.

He doesn't turn to face me. "You don't like chicken masala?"

"You're the one who's been cooking. The French toast. That was you?"

A quiet laugh. "You finished it off, so I as- sumed it was to your liking."

The fact that this man can cook at all seems strange. This man who once roasted fish he caught from a lake with only dirt and stones and twigs to help him. Then again maybe that's exactly why he knows how to cook. Because he makes himself delicious food without any help at all.

"I thought you'd have a chef. Maybe someone famous. With a few cookbooks published, that kind of thing."

"No chefs. I could never trust one enough to eat what they make."

That's some intense paranoia. Then again, knowing the city and its vagaries, it might be a valid fear. "You could hire a tester," I say, cautiously walking into the room. The whole place seems strange to me, even though I've worked in diners and the Emerald's kitchen for years now. The diner had surly cooks. The Emerald, somewhat snooty chefs. I have no idea how to quantify Damon as a creator of comfort and art. It goes against all my experiences of cooking. He seems... relaxed.

"Poison isn't always immediate," he says to my tester idea. "Besides, what if he did drop dead? How would I ever find someone to replace him?"

I scrunch my nose at Damon, scooting onto one of the empty barstools that circle the island. "I guess that's kind of morbid, the whole idea of a tester."

"Not any more morbid than a bodyguard. They're putting their life on the line."

"Bodyguards like Hiro."

He glances at me. "You met her."

"She seems competent. And a little bit scary."

"Those are the actual job requirements for her position."

"Do you really think I need security? Isn't the Den secure?"

"Yes, but there's someone working who I don't trust."

"Who?" Realization hits me before the word

fully leaves my mouth. "Oh."

"Yes," he says. "Your father had access to the Den, to my businesses. Access to me. And that makes him a liability now that he's gone missing."

Unease stirs in my stomach. "Something could have happened to him. The same way something could have happened to Avery."

Damon sends me a dark look. "Do you really believe that? That your father is kidnapped in some basement, at the whim of a sexual predator?"

Tears sting my eyes, imagining Avery that way. "No."

"I don't think so either," he says, a little softer.

"But even if my father started gambling again, how would that mean I'm in danger?"

Damon takes his time about answering, seasoning the sauce that he's working on. After a moment I realize he might not answer at all. Then he dips a wooden spoon into the pot and carries it to me.

"Blow," he murmurs.

I blow a stream of air over the steaming spoon. When he pushes the spoon closer I open my lips and take a sip. Spice blooms on my tongue, making me close my eyes. "God, that's good."

When I open my eyes again Damon is looking at me with a strange intensity. "I meant what I said before. The problem with someone gambling isn't about the money. It's about the addiction."

"I know," I say, remembering every card game, every cheat.

Every desperate win so that we could eat that night.

Damon takes a sip from the same spoon, in the same place that I did. "He used you before, Penny. He used you to count cards. To clean up his mess. What's to say he won't use you again?"

My chest constricts. "He wouldn't."

Except that's a lie, and both of us know it. Hiro isn't here to protect me from the city in general. She's here to protect me from my own father.

The man I came back to the city to find.

And where does that leave Avery?

"I solved part of the code." The words come out before I've planned them.

Damon turns to face me, his expression blank. "You did."

"It says *COME ALONE*. There's still a bottom row of numbers I haven't figured out yet. It doesn't conform to the polynomial curve like the top part."

"I see."

"*COME ALONE.* What do you think it means? I mean, I guess it's obvious what it means. That we should come alone." I'm babbling now, my wits scattered thinking about Avery at the mercy of this mysterious code-maker. "But who do you think sent it?"

"No idea," he says, but with shadowy insight I realize it's a lie. He knows more than he's telling me. About my father. About Avery. He knows things that might even help solve the rest of the code, but he lets me scribble away in the dark.

CHAPTER EIGHTEEN

THE NEXT DAY I can't seem to focus. The numbers swim in front of my eyes. The worst part of this is not knowing whether I'm actually making headway. There are an infinite number of possibilities with even this bottom row, and I won't know whether I've hit the right one until I try it. Maybe not even then, if I don't recognize the message. This might not even *be* a message. Just random numbers meant to drive me insane.

I fumble through my tote bag to find my phone. It's almost out of battery, so I plug it into the wall before dialing Smith College's main number.

"Dr. Stanhope please," I tell the operator.

The phone rings, and for a moment I think he must be out of his office. It's the weekend so it's hit-or-miss whether he'd be there. He works on his research nonstop, but he can do it from home.

"Hello?" He sounds breathless.

"Are you okay?"

An uneven laugh. "Going for a run while the campus is quiet. I heard the phone ringing down the hallway." A pause, and he sounds more steady. "I hoped it was you."

"You did?"

"Fishing for compliments?"

I flush, realizing it's probably the truth. "I'm sorry."

"It's not a hardship to compliment you, Penny. But I'm more interested in hearing how you're doing right now. Are you okay? The whole campus is talking about Avery James."

"Do they have any leads?"

"Not that they're sharing publicly. I know you two were close."

Now I wonder whether we were close enough. Was there something she wanted to tell me? Something she was afraid of? "I'm working on something that might be related."

"With the police?"

"Not exactly. There's this message." My throat closes. "Well, it's a long number."

"You think it's a cipher?"

"Maybe. I've been working on it for a couple days, but I haven't gotten anywhere."

"Send it to me."

I hesitate. "I'm not sure—"

"That's what I did my graduate research in. Cryptanalysis."

"Wait. Really? I didn't know that."

"I started studying Ramsey numbers as an offshoot." He gives a small wry laugh. "Didn't expect my career to go in that direction, but the applications are really endless. And far more commercial."

"Commercial," I say, my forehead tightening.

"Sure. Even when you're working with governments, it's on the civil side. Utilities. And there's privatization all the time. Cell phone carriers. Internet data usage."

Something uncomfortable stirs in my chest. Once I had a terrible crush on this man. I thought he was the life I was supposed to have, the kind of man who would keep me safe. "I thought you were interested in the welfare system."

"Of course I am. They're basically the end cases, the place where reality proves or disproves theory. Anyway, this isn't the time. I can go on for hours about that, but we're talking about codes."

I flip the call to speakerphone so that I can snap a picture of the code. Something keeps me from sending it to him. Why am I hesitating when he can help? Even if he didn't have a strong background in cryptography he's a world-renowned mathematician—of course I value his insight.

And still I stare at the numbers on my phone screen, a knot in my throat.

How did I become so sure the message was in the arrangement of the numbers? What if the number represents a single entity? What if it's a direction—like a phone number? The number of digits aren't right, but the idea hooks into me. So many digits.

Not a social security number.

"Penny?" comes the voice from far away—from a different state, a different version of me. He isn't the life I'm supposed to have, which leaves me empty, adrift. Alone.

"One sec," I whisper.

It could be an ISBN number.

A quick Internet search pulls up an outdated textbook in oceanography. It's possible that's the answer, but it doesn't feel right. Dr. Stanhope wouldn't understand about gut instinct, but growing up in the west side, I learned to trust it. There's something here, not words within the number. Something the number points me to.

"Penny, when are you coming home?"

The words startle me enough that I lose my

train of thought. "Home?"

"Yes, home. Smith College. This is where you belong."

What a strange idea, that I belong there. That I belong anywhere. I always felt like an imposter at college, like someone would rip away my notebook and messenger bag and expose me for the poor trailer-park trash that I really am.

"I'm not sure. I have to find Avery before I can come back."

"You can't put your life on hold for her," he says, gently chiding.

That suddenly strikes me as wildly cruel. "Why can't I? She's my friend. One of my only friends. It's because of her that I got to go to Smith at all."

"Penny," he says, and I realize that I'm hysterical.

I should stop this. Hang up the phone. Find some way to act like a normal human instead of this sobbing, shaking mass of emotion, but I've been holding it together too long. "Oh God. She's gone. I have to do something. What can I do?"

"You are doing something," he reminds me.

The cipher. The terrible code. A horrible game where her life is at stake. It's not so different from playing poker from someone's life. Callous and wrong and so deeply a part of Tanglewood's stained fabric that it will never come out.

I force myself to breathe in slow, deep breaths. Losing it might feel better to me, but it doesn't help Avery at all. I need to be strong for her. "Talk to me more about the commercial uses of Ramsey numbers," I say.

There's a startled pause, where he's probably wondering if I've gone crazy. But if there's one thing I can rely on, it's Dr. Stanhope's passion for his work.

"There's this contract I'm working on in conjunction with the major digital radio supplier. They aren't bound by the same rules and restrictions as broadcast radio, so it's really the Wild West of communications policy."

Any other time I might find his enthusiasm endearing, but I'm staring at the number.

"Keep going."

"Are you sure you're okay, Penny?"

"You said something about Internet data usage."

"Right, well. There's the more obvious applications, in terms of the pricing for data plans and what's most profitable for the carriers. But the more interesting application is in distribution of the Internet itself. Each hub is a resource, so how do you utilize it best? How do you prioritize requests for usage?"

"If hubs are the resource, then people are the users?"

"More than that. Nowadays each person has multiple devices. Phones, tablets. Laptops. Each one vying for the same resources."

"An IP address," I whisper.

"Yes, that's right. The IP addresses are locations."

Excitement beats in my chest. "So an IP address is unique?"

"Penny, what does this have to do with Avery James?"

"Maybe everything."

I hold up the paper to the light and squint at the bottom row. It's the only part that isn't contained by the equation. There are little, almost imperceptible dots between some of the numbers. Not made with ink. They're imperfections in the paper, as if it was made for this purpose, to send this specific message. These wouldn't have shown up on pictures, not even high-resolution ones.

And that means we have a location. We know where to go.

Chapter Nineteen

WATER RUNS OVER my skin, hot and cleansing. This is the rush that I long for, the one that keeps me up late at night, the one I get every time I solve a problem. The more difficult the proof, the bigger the high. I'm actually jittery with relief, unable to keep my hands still.

Part of me knows there's more work to do—that we still have to track down the IP address and then follow the location. Part of me knows all that might not even lead to Avery, but this was my part to do. This was my personal mountain to climb, and I made it to the top.

For that I deserve to be clean, at least.

I let the hot spray from multiple nozzles drench me again and again.

A *boom* is my only warning before the bathroom door slams open.

Damon marches into the large bathroom, his wrath licking at my skin like flames, making the

THE QUEEN

water turn to steam. I shriek as he reaches for the glass door and slides it open.

"What are you doing?" I demand, trying to cover myself with my hands.

He's been angry before, in that devilish way, the one with smooth words and biting wit. That's not the man breathing hard in front of me. He looks more animal than person. "Why the fuck did you call Gabriel?"

"I called Nina," I say before I can think through my story. Before I even realize I need a story. "She left her phone number and told me to call her if I found anything."

A sound more like a snarl than a laugh bounces off the tiles. "Yes, I'm sure she did say that. What I want to know is what on earth possessed you to actually do it."

Water streams into my eyes, and they feel like tears. I hate that this man can make me cry, even fake shower tears. "She cares about finding Avery."

"She cares about running Gabriel's little fucking kingdom while he's busy handling his hard-on."

I don't know enough about the dynamics to argue the point, and I'm struck with a sudden panic that I've made a terrible mistake. This is my problem. It's *always* my problem.

No matter how well I understand numbers, people remain a complete and utter mystery. They're black boxes. Unknowns. I don't understand what happens inside them. I don't understand what's happening inside Damon as he stares at me, frustration rolling off him in freezing waves.

My throat feels tight. "She knew about computers. About programming. And the number—it wasn't a code. It was an IP address. I confirmed the pattern matches someplace in the United States, but not more than that. I thought she could find it."

"She found it," he says grimly.

"Did she find Avery?"

A hoarse laugh. "I very much doubt it. Unless Avery has been checked into a high-security mental hospital. Because that's where the IP address came from."

I blink through the hot sting. "Why?"

"You asked me why I don't consider Gabriel Miller my friend. This is why. Because that mental hospital? That's where my father lives."

A flash of terror, the water rising, blackness closing in. "I thought he was dead."

"Of course you did. You would put down an

animal like that when you have the chance, right? That's the logical thing to do. No cure for rabies. No cure for being a psychopath either."

I blink through the hot sting. "I don't understand. Is Gabriel working with him?"

"That's one way of putting it, though he wouldn't agree. No, Avery was touched to realize her father was still alive. Despite what he did to her. What he did to *you*. And she thought it was some kind of noble act to leave him alive."

I shake my head, horrified by the idea. That sounds like something Avery would care about—nobility. Honor. She will always be the heiress to the Tanglewood fortune, no matter what happened to her father's money. It's in her upbringing. Her very blood.

For me it's always been different—not a question of nobility but survival.

"Why didn't you—" My voice breaks.

"Kill him anyway? What a great idea. One I've considered many times. Except that Gabriel made it clear that the man—my fucking father—was under his protection now."

I suck in a sharp breath, stunned by the betrayal. Gabriel may have had noble intentions in letting Jonathan Scott live, but protect him from Damon? That went too far. Damon is the person most hurt by his father. The person with the scars to prove it.

"And you valued your friendship too much to make a move against him."

I don't need to see the bitter agreement in his eyes to know the truth. Damon may pretend he doesn't give a damn. He'll laugh at the sky as it sends lightning down around him. But he does care.

"A lot of good that did," he says darkly. "If he hurt Avery in the end."

"But why would he give us his IP address? Why would he send us that message?"

"Of course he wants us to know. He's all alone in the middle of a fucking fortress with no one but the little orderlies and nurses and patients to bat around with his claws. I told Gabriel that place couldn't hold him. No place can."

"He's showing us that he has access to the internet," I realize out loud. "He's taunting us."

"More than that, sweet Penny. He's summoning us."

Urgency beats against my ribs, because I already sense his refusal in the air. "Then we have to go. If he's behind Avery's disappearance, we have to go and make him tell us where she is. Or what if she's there with him? If he has the ability to send messages like that, he can do anything. Even kidnap her. We have to leave."

"I don't have to do a damn thing," Damon says.

Shock holds me breathless. "What?"

"I learned to ignore my father a long time ago. It's called survival, sweetheart, and I'm not about to stop now. Not even for a long-lost sister I barely know."

"How can you talk like that about her?"

"She made her choice when she kept him alive. I warned her. I told her and Gabriel exactly what would happen, and look, here we are. Surprise."

It's both shocking and painful to see him be so casual about the very real danger she's in. I think I'm finally seeing the fabled Damon Scott who took over the criminal underworld of Tanglewood. This is the man people fear. The one they plead with and hide from and threaten like an animal backed into a corner. The man who owns loan markers for some of the most powerful people in the city, who owns strip clubs and dirty businesses. He didn't get to this place on his half-smile and sharp suits alone. There's something sinister in him, and I'm witnessing it now.

Anger warms me despite his chilly words. "Then I'll go."

His gaze lowers to my body, a long look that covers every shadow, every curve. My hands barely cover my breasts, between my legs. Most of me is exposed, and he makes sure I feel it. He makes sure I feel how powerless I am in this moment—that I can't help Avery, that I can't even help myself.

"No, Penny. You aren't going anywhere."

Chapter Twenty

THE BEAT STARTS up at nine p.m., which seems early. I don't know how invitations are handled for wild sex parties—an X-rated vellum strip with calligraphy? A secret Facebook group for the rich and depraved? However it happens, people spill out of cabs and black limos, dressed in sparkly clothes and shiny leather that will no doubt come off soon. Last night the street had been clear; tonight the Den is the host of the town.

There's a sick feeling in my stomach, because this party is pointed.

It's a message as real as the slip of paper with a number scribbled on it. One that says Damon Scott answers to no one, not even his father. Especially not his father.

It says he isn't going to help Avery, as plain as day.

Not an especially hard cipher, this one. A sex-drenched *fuck you.*

Hiro leans against the banister in the darkened hallway, watching the crowd mill around. I join her, leaning my elbows on carved wood. Most people still have their clothes on. They're dancing, drinking. Laughing. It's hard to imagine feeling that kind of reckless joy. It's too foreign to even want it, like watching a flock of birds fly overhead. They're beautiful, but I know better than to fly.

"I'm afraid to ask," I say softly. "Are you here to keep me in the room?"

"My instructions are to keep anyone else out."

"So if I go downstairs..."

"I would follow you. At a discreet distance, of course."

I look down at her clothes, the same black shirt and blazer, the same utilitarian jeans and black boots. She will fit into this crowd of glitz and glamour about as well me.

My Smith College T-shirt and black yoga pants are variations of what I packed in my suitcase. There aren't any party dresses or slinky skirts.

Walking downstairs feels a little like being Cinderella, except without the fairy godmother. I'm showing up in rags and chimney soot. Bare feet instead of a golden-white carriage.

People stop their conversation when they see me. They stop laughing.

Which is ironic, because I probably look pretty funny.

When I reach the ground floor, there's actually a little crowd formed, waiting for me. They show no intention of moving, openly gawking, blocking my path. Until Hiro steps behind me. Whatever expression she wears on her face, it makes everyone take a step back. Then another.

That's how I plow a path between people, to where Damon's makeshift throne was the first night. Sure enough he's holding court there again, reclined in a large leather armchair while women and men dance around him. No matter that they're beautiful. Damon looks almost bored.

Until he sees me at the other end of the room. Then his expression turns anticipatory. That's never a good thing when you're dealing with a man like him. Nothing he looks forward to will be good for me.

If I'm a broke-down version of Cinderella, Damon is a very dark prince.

"Come here," he says with a crook of his finger.

Of course I was coming to see him anyway. Now it's like he ordered me to do it. I take a step closer, wondering if I'm crazy for confronting him. Hiding in my room won't very well help either. I have to do something. Hiro melts into the crowd, and I'm on my own.

I keep going until I'm a foot away from him, all the people hushed around us.

"What are you doing?" I demand.

"Enjoying myself," he says with a little smile.

I've seen him leaning over me for a kiss. I've seen him peruse my body with a hungry gaze. That's what Damon Scott looks like when he's having a good time. This is something else. He's not enjoying himself while he knows Avery is in his father's grip. "That's a lie."

He grasps my wrist before I realize he's reaching for me, and I tumble into his lap. "It's a little better now that you're here. And now that you're close."

My muscles are tense, stiff, as I control my natural instinct to fight him. I want to slap him for touching me. No, I want to slap him for touching me *in front of these strangers.* For turning the terrible, irrepressible attraction between us into a public affair.

That would prove that it matters to me. That *he* matters to me.

I lean back in his arms, pretending I'm unconcerned with my yoga pants and my bare feet. Pretending I'm as comfortable with my sexuality as the people watching us with betrayal and envy. "I don't think you're enjoying yourself at all. I think you're pretending. Which is interesting."

"That's not interesting. I'm much more interested in what brought you downstairs. Is there something you wanted to see, sweet girl? Something you want to try?"

"How about honesty?"

A low laugh. "Honestly, you're the most beautiful woman I've ever seen."

The words make a mockery of my request. They make of a mockery of *me*, a regular girl surrounded by women that belong on magazine covers. One of them gives a delicate little snort.

I want to pretend like he hasn't hurt me, but my cheeks heat. "We should be going to find Avery."

"You could argue that she brought this on herself. She's the one who wanted him to live."

"How dare you? No one asks for that." In the second that passes we're no longer talking about Avery but about me. About what his father did to me. I still feel his hands on my skin, bruises like brands.

Damon tenses underneath me, but his voice

sounds casual as he says, "Avery made her bed. Now let her lie in it. Meanwhile you can lie in my bed."

Now I do struggle against him, but his arm is like iron across my lap. "Let me go."

A commotion from the front door disrupts the crowd, and Damon tightens his hold even farther. Gabriel Miller is always in control, always in charge, a businessman with an air of danger and more money than God. Now he looks haggard as he pushes through the crowd.

"You," he says on a snarl.

Damon sets me upright before I realize what's happening, standing and pushing me behind him in one smooth move. "Oh, did you get the text message? How nice of you to join us."

"Don't do this," Gabriel says, his voice low and a little desperate.

"I'm not doing anything," Damon says, almost playful as he objects.

"This is Avery we're talking about. She's—" The large man breaks off, his golden eyes glinting with danger and emotion.

"Avery can take care of herself. Probably."

"I could fucking kill you right now. Not one person here would stop me."

Damon's voice is wry. "Of course not. It

would be the best entertainment they've had all year."

"I should do it," Gabriel says on a rumble that sends chills through me. For a breathless moment violence flashes in his golden eyes. It passes in a rush, leaving only desolation.

"Then do it," Damon says softly. "Kill me if you have to, but don't come here and talk to me like you have any right. That's what you lost. That's what you gave up for her."

He strides past us, and everyone returns to their dancing and their sex. The show is over, except for a desperate Gabriel. "Talk to him," he says.

My eyes widen. "He doesn't listen to me."

"He does. You're the only one." His laugh is thick with grief.

"What are you going to do?"

"Go there myself, of course. But Damon was right when he said no place can hold his father. And that means we'll need him. One way or another he has to come."

CHAPTER TWENTY-ONE

ORDINARY PEOPLE ARE a puzzle, but Damon is the only one who's ever interested me. The only one I wish I could solve. And never more than right now, as the darkness sets in.

It takes me a few days to realize that he's serious about not going. I think I actually go through the first two stages of grief—denial, when I'm sure he's secretly packing his bags and heading to the airport. Anger, when I consider dumping the eggs benedict that appears outside my door on his sleepy, beautiful body where it reclines in bed.

Then I get to bargaining, and it feels like more than a stage. It feels like the answer.

This is what Damon understands in his bones, the way other children know about love or security. He understands the value of the gamble. The value of pushing your chips in.

And that's what he wants from me.

For me to put something in the center of the table. Otherwise you don't get to play. He's not going to see Avery until I do something. Until I offer him something.

It's the third night that I emerge from the room, once he's turned off the light and gone to bed. The glow from a tablet lights him in bed. He masks his surprise quickly, setting the tablet aside. "What are you doing awake?"

I don't answer him. I'm not sure I have the nerve to speak right now. I couldn't say *I'll trade my body for the chance to save Avery.* Couldn't say, *you can have sex with me if you go see your father.* There's only exactly enough nerve to stand at the foot of the bed.

It's like I've been waiting for him my entire life, since I was that six-year-old girl.

He's here, sitting in front of me.

And not here, his mind still held captive by the years that came before.

The lamp on my desk casts a spotlight on him, on his tattoos with their tragic story and his body with its terrible beauty. I see the endless lines of ink etched into him. Monsters with only one eye. A wild woman with snakes for hair. And waves for miles of muscle.

Already he's seen me naked. Worse than that, he's seen me broken and bleeding. Somehow it's still painful to reach for the hem of my shirt.

Excruciating to lift enough to reveal the thin band of my stomach. Heartbreaking to watch him study me with cold desire.

I hesitate when it's halfway up my body, suddenly afraid.

Does he know what's at stake? Of course he does.

"Tomorrow?" I ask, hating how much my voice trembles.

Tomorrow we'll go see Jonathan Scott. We'll answer the summons, the cipher. Tomorrow we try to find Avery. Damon doesn't exactly agree. Nothing as bland as *yes* or *it's a deal.*

"Come here," he says instead.

How many times has he asked that of me? When he was lying in that bed or when he reclined in the chair downstairs. I never did come. Not the way I do now, hitching my leg onto the bed, pulling my T-shirt off all the way. It lands in an unceremonious heap on the crisp white sheets.

I'm kneeling beside him, unsteady on the solid mattress.

He could fall on me. It would make this easier, but Damon Scott doesn't do easy.

My bra is plain and cotton the way all my bras are. I buy them in packs at the big box store. They're all the same, all boring, all completely unsexy. They should be a turn-off after the sequins and lace he's seen downstairs, but I think I've solved this part of the puzzle.

Lingerie and high heels, perfectly pouting lips—they're an invitation. What sane man would turn them down? Except Damon Scott isn't sane. He's perverse, and he wants *this*. A chaste white bra that no other man has seen. Pale white skin that no light has touched.

I fumble in my nervousness. The clasp is a needle and a thread, my hands as large as tree trunks.

Damon watches me with unerring patience. It's part of my payment, his patience. My hands behind my back, working, working. Making me embarrass myself for him, a far deeper cost than pleasuring him.

The clasp unlocks in the back. The cups fall forward, leaning away from my breasts.

As if that unlocks him, he reaches a hand out. One finger down the center of my chest. He tugs the bra away completely. The cool air touches my nipples, turns them tight.

He traces the plump circle of my breast with light fingertips. His hand looks massive in front of me. Or maybe that's just that I'm small. It's like he's measuring me—and I already know I'll come up short. That's the point. That's the payment, but I find myself stuttering.

"I'm—I'm not—"

He doesn't pause in his light perusal. "You're not what?"

"Sexy."

My high school boyfriend liked that I never demanded anything from him. Dr. Stanhope likes that I'm clever. Maybe I should be satisfied with those things, but they aren't passion. They aren't hunger.

Silver flashes through Damon's dark eyes. "Who told you that?"

In the end it's not Brennan or Dr. Stanhope who made me afraid of sex. It's the man we're going to see tomorrow. Green tiles and black soil. Deep roots that I can never escape. "I'm just saying, you don't have to touch me. I don't know exactly what to do, but if you tell me, I'll do it."

"You think I don't want to touch you," he says flatly.

"I don't want you to pretend."

He flips me over on the bed, so I'm looking up at him. "Let me make this very clear. No other woman has been in this bed. You're the only one here. The only one I've ever wanted here."

I know my eyes widen, know my breath stutters out of me, but he doesn't acknowledge my shock. Doesn't seem to care as he leans forward to press a kiss on the side of my neck.

There's a switch in that inch of skin; that's what I realize as my body arches in sudden tension. He doesn't acknowledge that either. It's with grim determination that he maps every inch of my chest with his mouth, that he feels me before he tastes. That he closes his mouth over my nipple. Flicks his tongue until I make a keening sound.

Damon isn't the kind of man to tell me false platitudes, but if I doubted the truth of his words, he proves them with the thoroughness he shows my breasts—as if he could stay here all night, kissing me, biting me. Making my body writhe. It's minutes, hours, an eternity later that I realize my body is moving in a specific rhythm. The same way I move my hand between my legs at night.

When he hooks his hand into the waistband of my pants and pulls them down, it's an unspeakable relief. The heat is too much, the friction incendiary. Only, he leaves my panties on. White and plain. From the same metal rack as my bras. He presses kisses along the cheap seam, across my stomach and down my thighs. With a rough hand he shoves my legs apart, pressing his face against my dampness.

"Does this feel like pretending?" he asks, his voice dark.

It takes me a moment to realize what he means. My words. "No," I whisper.

"Good," he says, levering himself to look at me. "No lies between us. Not tonight."

Complete honesty. I don't think I'm ready for that. He definitely isn't, no matter what he thinks. There are things floating in my head that would send him running. *I'm afraid. Don't hurt me. I love you.*

It's not only words that have truth. It's touch. I cup his cheek in my hand, feeling his bristly jaw against my palm, taking his tension into my body. Then I curve my hand around his neck and draw him down.

A kiss. Is it possible to lie with your lips and tongue pressed together?

Is it possible to stand apart with your heartbeats attuned to one?

I'm not experienced enough to know, but the way he leans down to meet me, the way my body instinctively cradles his, it feels like a truth so deep I'm uncovering it instead of saying it.

He rears back, tugging my panties down my

legs. He has no mercy when he spreads my legs—wide. Very wide. Is this normal? The way he studies me, as if trying to memorize every pink and every shadow?

I move my hands to cover myself. "Damon."

"Penny." It's a plea that he ignores. Or maybe not ignores. One that he refuses, implacable, picking up my hands, pressing my wrists into the bed beside my body.

"It's too much."

"Why do you think I let you wait so long?"

The question holds a thousand implications.

It's a patchwork I would need time to unravel, a cipher I need to study and decode, but he doesn't give me time. He gives me his mouth against my sex, right up the center with the flat of his tongue. I make a squeak at the end, where he lingers at the peak of my body.

"Wait," I moan.

That makes him laugh a little, a vibration I feel right against my clit. "What are we waiting for?" he asks, mocking. "For you to come? That won't be long, sweet girl."

He touches me, one finger combined with his tongue. It's enough to send ripples of pleasure through my body. Enough to give truth to his words. Disproving the terrible secret I couldn't admit, even to myself—that I didn't know truth could feel good.

I want to touch him. To run my hands along the terrain of him—to feel the unlikely smoothness where ink hasn't left a mark, to touch the silver-white scars that have. He shakes his head slowly, pressing my hands into the mattress. "No."

"Why not?"

"Because we're doing truth tonight."

Any other night he would give me that arrogant half smile. He would invite me into his bed with complete unconcern, as if women climb in every night instead of never.

"Okay." It's the hardest thing I've had to do, keeping my hands against the mattress.

He could make a joke of this submission, but he's strangely grave. "Thank you."

Then he presses his mouth to my core, making me squirm and scream. His tongue knows every magic secret place on my body; his lips guide the way. His teeth glance my tender spots, making fear spark behind my eyelids. My body bows up toward him; it squirms away. I'm a puppet, his talented fingers my string. And God, he pulls and pulls.

A sheen of sweat covers me. Between my legs

it's slick from my own juices and his mouth. It's indecent, the way I'm spread out. Unthinkable, the way I want to stay here.

When he pulls away for the millionth time, I make a frustrated sound.

From his knowing laugh I can tell he's doing it on purpose. Deprivation. Torture. A physical ache so real and so acute my body squirms and pants even when he's not touching me. Especially then.

"Please, Damon." The words burst out of me, shaming me. There's no such thing as dignity beneath his mouth and hands and benevolent gaze.

"You can leave anytime," he says, challenge in his tone.

He wants me to run away, to undo the deal I made with him, the very devil. That he would help Avery for the price of my body. Probably this was his plan all along, as he watched me take off my T-shirt. When he waited for me to fumble with the bra clasp. He knew he would make me burn. That he'd make me beg.

"I'm not going anywhere," I promise, breathless.

"Good," he murmurs, lowering his mouth to my stomach and down, down. "Because now I've had a taste. If you run, I'll chase you."

His mouth descends on me again, licking deep inside me, his tongue so soft it hurts. It's suffering, being made to lie open and vulnerable while he's coated in armor. The clothes don't matter now. His armor comes from his tattoos and his scars. It comes from the way he controls my body, moving me, pleasuring me, bending me to his will.

He finds my clit with his eyes closed in pleasure, as if he prefers to move by touch rather than sight. He makes me jump. "Too much," I gasp.

It seems to be the signal he was waiting for, because he does it again. And again. The point of his tongue sweeping circles around my clit, tighter and tighter. Spiraling toward the center until I'm beyond begging, past words. There's only the urgent rhythm of my body, humping his mouth upward in a desperate plea for friction, for release, for anything.

His finger pushes inside me, then another, twisting in a way that makes me pant. There's not enough air in the large room, in the Den, only smoke and sounds and twisted promises.

His touch is enough to make my body crazy, but it's his eyes that I need.

When his midnight eyes watch me, I come

apart. Wild pulses. Muscles clenching and pulsing so hard it hurts. My whole body overtaken, but my gaze never leaves his. It feels like giving something to him, spilling pleasure out like I'll never be able to find it again. The boundaries so blurred I'm not sure I'll ever be able to build them back up again.

CHAPTER TWENTY-TWO

IN THE AFTERMATH the air is moist and salt, an ocean made of our bodies, a sky made from panting breaths. I've imagined sex a hundred thousand times—all of them with Damon Scott. My dreams came up with equations, the things he would do to me, the things he would take.

My dreams could never come up with this.

I'm blind in these deep waters. Not helpless. I reach for him, feeling along burning skin and clenching muscles. When I find the right place, his whole body shudders. The sound of his gasped breath embeds itself inside me, fitting into some place with its exact shape.

He grasps my wrist hard enough to make me squeak. "No, Penny."

For a moment I struggle with him, tugging at my hand as if I have a chance of dislodging him. As if I'm the one calling the shots right now. Only when I give up does he gently push my hand away.

My throat swells. "Did I do it wrong?"

An uneven laugh. "Are you capable of doing things wrong? That's something I'd like to see."

"Then why can't I touch you?"

"Because that isn't what I want from you."

This is a game. I knew that. I thought I knew that... but somehow there's an ache in my chest. There's more at stake than my body. *My heart.*

The pleasure I felt is still here, no longer euphoria, but something darker.

"You don't want me to touch you," I say, more stunned than I have a right to be. "You don't want me to kiss you. Or suck you. Or do anything to you."

"That's right, Penny. Now run away to your little room."

I look at his lap, where the sheet tents an erection so large it would be terrifying if I thought he were going to do anything with it. "Will you touch yourself after?"

He grins. "Do you want to watch? Or maybe you'd like me to make you come again."

Everything is a game with him, but I'm struck by the realization that it's all a cover. A cover for what? For the fact that *nothing* is a game to him? That he cares too much?

"No," I say simply.

The pause between us weighs heavy. "Excuse me?"

"I said no. I'm not going to run away to my little room so that you can jack off while still tasting me. Maybe you're too shy to want me here, but I deserve to see this. And you deserve to let me."

I think I could have punched him in the face and he would have been less shocked. "Shy? Jesus Christ. You've seen the parties I have."

"And I've seen you, fully dressed in them. Watching but not participating."

He glances between my legs, where I can still feel the echo of his tongue. "And what about two minutes ago? I think I participated plenty, then."

"In a private room with the door locked. And you won't let me reciprocate."

His voice is pure venom. "A blow job, Penny. If you want to do it, you can at least say the words. You want to suck my cock. Say it."

I flush from his derision. "Fine, I want to suck your cock. But you won't let me. What are you afraid of? That I'll hurt you?"

"The only thing I'm afraid of is that I'll be bored out of my mind. I'm not only referring to the men and women at my parties. I own strip clubs, darling. In case you've forgotten. I know some of the most"—he smiles a little—"talented women in the city."

The more he tries to insult me, the more I see it as the distraction it's meant to be. "And how many of them have you actually slept with? How many of them have seen you vulnerable? How many of them have touched you?"

"None," he says on a hissed breath. "Is that what you want to hear?"

It's the truth; the certainty of that sinks inside me like poison. I've been trying to make him be honest with me for days. For years, even. Now that he's finally done it, all I feel is deep sorrow. "I'm sorry."

"Don't pity me, sweetheart. I've had my share of sex."

"The kind you wanted?" I ask softly.

Maybe another woman would be fooled. Maybe the people downstairs think Damon Scott has wild sex because he hosts parties at the Den, because he owns strip clubs.

I've seen Damon before he became this dashing stranger. I knew the wild boy who tried to run away from home. Angry, dangerous. Defensive. There are only a few ways teenage boys get like that.

"I'm not the only person Jonathan Scott has

hurt," I whisper.

"You're the only one he shouldn't have touched," he says, voice thick with remorse.

"I don't understand."

"He wanted to create a monster. And he's good at what he does."

I shake my head. "You did what you had to do to survive."

"I didn't just survive what he did to me. I thrived in it, understand? I became what he wanted me to be. Fuck, I was already a monster. Coming from that man. Being his son. I can't escape that."

"You can," I whisper urgently, my heart fractured at his agony.

"But you weren't part of that life. You were the one thing I wanted to be clean, to be safe. To be free from this city. Which is exactly why he targeted you. Don't you get that? I'm the reason he hurt you."

"I know, Damon. He told me, but that doesn't make it true."

A hoarse sound. "Everything you've suffered is because of me."

"Your father is responsible for what he does. I know you tried to keep people safe. You tried to keep *me* safe. You're still doing it. That's why I'm in that room, isn't it? Because someone would have to go through you to get to me."

"No one's getting to you," he says on a low growl.

"But you can't keep everyone safe all the time. That's not your responsibility."

"It is," he says, teeth clenched, and with shock I realize he means it. "I'm the only one who knows what he's truly capable of doing. The only one capable of stopping him."

My heart aches, because he's right. He's the only one who knows what Jonathan Scott is fully capable of—because he's suffered all of it. For years. Because no one stopped him. No one could. In a twisted way it's why he won't go after Avery, because he believes he can't save her. In his mind she's already lost. The dark place in my mind whispers that he might be right.

I touch my forefinger lightly to a darker patch of skin on the side of his abdomen, a few inches below the endless stylized waves. "Tell me about this one."

His eyes flash. "What are you doing?"

"Tell me."

"Cast iron," he says, his voice devoid of emotion. "A fireplace poker."

I can't quite control the flinch that comes

from imagining that. The wound has healed over, almost smooth to the touch. Which means it happened a very long time ago. How young was he?

Without commenting on it, I move to a thin white line of raised skin. "This one."

"Penny," he warns.

"If you tell me, then you won't be the only one who knows."

His breath hitches—I can't hear it or see it, but I feel the shift in his chest. "And you think I want that? You're the last person I want to burden with this."

"You keep trying to keep me safe, Damon Scott. No matter what it costs you."

"That's right. My life means nothing. It hasn't meant anything since I met a little girl who stole a hundred-dollar bill from my backpack because she was hungry."

Guilt burns like acid. "I'm sorry about that."

"Don't you get it, Penny? I would give you a thousand of those. I'd give you every dollar I have, and then steal even more if that's what you wanted."

"Why?" I whisper, suddenly afraid.

"God knows," he says, and it really does sound like a prayer. "My life would be so much simpler if I could just fuck one of those women down there. If I could just stop thinking about you for a single goddamn breath. Instead I've spent years taking over the fucking city so that I could give it you."

Words are caught in my throat. Words like *no* and *impossible* and *please.*

"And the worst part is, you don't want it, do you? You were never fooled by a suit and a smile, were you? You knew that only covered up a wild animal."

"That's not true," I say, but it is. God, it is.

"You wanted to leave Tanglewood, and you were right to. You don't belong here. So get back in your fucking little box, because that's where I'm going to keep you until I can send you away again."

I stand up from the bed like my limbs aren't shattered, like my body is still in one piece. Like his gaze isn't battering against my back. The small room is the same as when I left it. I'm the one who's different. I'm the one hollowed out, blackened. A husk of the girl who went looking for him.

CHAPTER TWENTY-THREE

I'M LYING AWAKE in bed when I hear the commotion downstairs. A man's shout. A disturbing *thump*. I peek out of my little room to find the large bed empty, the sheet thrown back. Is it Damon downstairs? Or did he already go down to investigate?

I find my answer at the bottom of the stairs.

Damon stands over a prone body. A large body. One covered in bruises and blood.

"Daddy," I whisper.

He looks up at me with one bloodshot eye, the other too puffy to see. "There you are. I had to make sure you were safe. Had to make sure—"

"Don't speak to her," Damon says, his voice bored.

It's a lie, that boredom. The casual look of him, loose pants and no shirt—that's a lie, too. Everything about this man is deliberate and honed. He's a blade, and the man on the floor in front of him is sliced into pieces.

I rush to Daddy's side, helping him stand. "You need to go to a hospital."

"No," he grunts, leaning on me. "No hospitals."

Damon gives a coarse laugh.

I glare at him. "Did you do this to him?"

"He deserves what happened to him. Worse, actually."

How can my father's weight feel both heavy and painfully frail at the same time? He seems to have aged a hundred years since I saw him last. "Daddy," I whisper. "What did you do?"

He groans. "I made a mistake."

"A mistake," Damon says, mocking. "Is that what the kids are calling it these days?"

Daddy shudders in my arms, and I lead him to one of the large leather chairs, sending Damon a dirty look. I know that I have no power here, not really. Only what he gives me. I still dare him to tell me no. That Daddy can't sit down, that this broken man can't rest here.

Damon leans against the wall, indolent and muscular, as if unconcerned with any of this.

I hold two larger hands in mine, terribly aware of all the times this has happened before. The chair was a lumpy armchair instead of leather, the floor thin carpet instead of an oriental rug. But the feeling is the same—the searing disappointment that my father has once again hit the bottom.

And here I am, kneeling with him. Always with him.

"I started again," he says roughly. "I didn't mean to. Not at first. It was only one game in the Cellar. Old friends, you know. And someone new."

"It's never one game, Daddy."

He sighs. "I know. I should never have sat down at the table again. And then next thing you know I'm down five large."

I manage not to flinch, but maybe that's because this is too familiar. How can something that's happened so many times still hurt so much?

"I think I could have done it, you know," he continues. "I could have paid the money on the salary I was getting and still covered your tuition."

"Why didn't you?" I ask, my voice hollow. I know the answer. Addiction.

"You," he says softly.

My gaze snaps to his watery brown eyes. "What?"

"The new guy, I didn't even catch his name that night. Can you believe it? He shows up at my door the next night. Says he'll tell Damon I'm gambling again, that I'm in debt. That was against the rules. He was real firm about that from the beginning."

"Loyalty," Damon says softly. "It doesn't divide. Like an atom, the smallest unit of matter. It can't be split apart. If it's not with me, it's with someone else."

My father doesn't look up. "This man says, all I have to fix it is call you home for a visit."

I blink at him. "Why would he want that?"

"I don't know," he says slowly. "Not for sure. But I think... I think it's because you mean something to Damon Scott. Or at least he believed you do. And he would have hurt you. He would have used you as leverage. And I couldn't do that to you. Not when I've already hurt you so much."

You mean something to Damon Scott.

I swallow hard. "What did you do?"

"I panicked. I thought maybe I could make the money back, pay it and no one would know the difference. I took out loans, gambled it all away. It turned out like it always did, Penny. And then I was so ashamed.... God, I didn't know what to do."

Damon pushes off the wall, prowling behind me. "Whoever this asshole is, he went through enough trouble to find your old gambling spot, to get your buddies to lure you back, and to make sure you lost. Even if you had made the money back, it wouldn't have helped. He didn't want that."

"Daddy," I whisper. "Who was this man?"

"I don't know. I'd never met him before." He shudders. "His eyes, though. There was something not right about his eyes. I knew not to look at him directly, even during the game. There was something... insane about him."

A cold finger runs down my spine. *Insane.*

Daddy shakes his head. "The Russians, I borrowed money from them. When they found me tonight, I thought they were going to kill me. Instead they roughed me up and brought me here."

"I had to call in quite a favor for that," Damon says on a drawl.

My eyes widen, and I turn back to look at him. "You saved him?"

"'Saved' is such a strong word."

"Why did you say you had beaten him?"

"I merely said that he deserved what he got. You made your assumptions."

The air feels thin. "So what happens now?"

"Nothing," Damon says, sounding weary.

"Things will go back to the way they were. Your father will lay low until I can pay his debts."

He leaves the room without even a goodbye. Daddy slumps as soon as he's out of sight, clearly having used the reserves of his energy. He needs medical attention. Or at least rest. But I can't stop myself from running after Damon.

I catch him halfway up the stairs. "Wait."

He pauses, not quite turned toward me. Not quite turned away. "Yes?"

"Why did you bid on my father? If loyalty is so important to you, if he has a history of gambling. Why did you even want to win him in the first place? Why did you make that bet with me?"

A shake of his head, almost a helpless gesture from such a capable man. "You know the answer to that, baby genius. Because it was the only way I could help you. And you don't just mean something to me. You mean everything. Understand? Every goddamn thing."

As if he didn't just shatter my world and put it back together, he heads upstairs.

I stay at the bottom, staring up at him for a long time before tending my father's wounds, lost in contemplation. Daddy's disappearance wasn't related to Avery after all. It's just the garden variety heartbreak of a man who chooses gambling over family. When does it end?

How does the cycle stop?

"Does he hurt you?" Daddy asks when I finish bandaging him.

Leaning back on my heels I consider the question. The emotional ache is almost unbearable, but can that really be on Damon's shoulders? Is it his fault if I want more of him than he can give? He doesn't owe me anything. Not like the man in front of me.

"You hurt me," I say gently.

He looks away, a familiar expression of shame on his ruddy face. "I'm sorry."

"Daddy."

I wait until he looks at me. "Don't come back." The words come out as tender as I can make them, as soft as I feel them. There's no victory in this moment, only resignation. "You aren't happy in this city. And you aren't safe. Leave and don't come back."

Chapter Twenty-Four

GET THE call when I'm thirty thousand feet in the air. My cell phone rings, and I fumble through my backpack. Damon doesn't even look away from the window, ignoring the phone call. Ignoring me.

He's hardly spoken to me at all except to tell me when the car would be arriving to take us to the airport. From there we boarded a private jet. Hiro sits in the back of the plane, her eyes closed, her body still. I might believe she's sleeping except that I sense a deep wariness around her.

Avery's face smiles up at me from the phone screen, and my heart skips a beat. I took that picture my first year at Smith when we met up for dinner. I cropped her face in the square, so you can't see Gabriel in the background. It's impossible to forget his expression, though—the mixture of tenderness and ferocity.

"Hello?" I ask cautiously.

A small sigh. "Penny. It's so good to hear your

voice."

My heart beats wildly in my chest. "God. It really is you. Are you okay? Are you safe?"

She hesitates. "Now I am. Gabriel is here with me. He told me you helped find me."

"What about...?" It's hard to even say his name, impossible to imagine him doing the things he did to me to Avery. I sprang up from between bricks, an unlikely weed. Being crushed beneath his boot wasn't pleasant, but it was the life that I was made for. Avery has delicate petals and beautiful color.

"Jonathan Scott," she says.

"Did he hurt you?"

"He hurt a lot of people." Her voice cracks. "Maybe you most of all. I'm sorry that I let him live. I thought it was the right thing to do, the noble thing, but I was wrong."

"Shhh." I wish I were with her right now to give her a hug. But if Jonathan Scott has had his hands on her, she might not want a hug from me. "Don't worry about that now."

"I am worried about it, because I think Gabriel's going to leave me."

"What?" If Gabriel leaves my friend for having been violated, for being a victim, I'm going to personally shoot him. Or at least tell him he's the worst kind of bastard.

"He's going to go back there. To kill Jonathan Scott in revenge, but he doesn't understand."

"What doesn't he understand?"

"Jonathan Scott did more than escape the asylum. He took it over. He had the nurses…" A loud sob escapes, before she steadies her breathing. "He had the nurses locked up in the rooms, naked. The inmates he could control worked for him as guards. The ones he couldn't, he killed."

My throat tightens. "Oh God."

"This is why Damon was so intent on killing him. He knew that he couldn't be locked up."

I glance at Damon, who's watching me with an intent expression, his dark eyes unfathomable. "Are you at the asylum?"

"We flew to Chicago. I'm actually in the hospital now, but I'm fine. A few bruises, that's all. Gabriel insisted on having a doctor look at me…before he flies back there. I don't want him to leave me. Even with a guard—"

"Of course he should stay with you."

"Jonathan Scott had these terrible games he would play with the inmates." She pauses, her voice thick. "That he would play with me. He thought they were too broken to fight back, and they almost were. I had to convince them that we could break free. That we could do it together."

Shock sinks into me. "You mean you escaped by yourself?"

"No," she says reasonably. "We all did."

Of course she would frame it that way. It's so like Avery—to lead a revolution and give credit to those she led. "When did Gabriel get there?"

"We went to the nearest town and walked into the police station like that, thirty women and men with only blankets and dirty feet. Gabriel had already landed at the airport and was driving to the asylum when I called him from the station."

"My God, Avery."

Her tone is grim. "I know. The FBI showed up and said they would handle Jonathan Scott, and I want to believe them, but look what he did to the mental hospital."

"Listen, Avery. Whatever he did to you..." I trail off, because I don't know how to comfort her. *It doesn't matter.* But it does matter. It means everything to be violated. Everything and nothing.

"Don't worry," she murmurs. "He did mess with my head, but not that way. He said I was his daughter. That he wanted to get the family back together."

And now Damon is on a plane headed toward him. That's exactly what Jonathan Scott knew would happen. He's pulling everyone's strings. "I'm sorry."

She gives a sad laugh. "Family. That's how he lured me out of the room, did you know that? Had this lookalike of my mother along the hillside in the moonlight. It was one of the inmates, but she looked so much like her."

"I had no idea. I woke up alone and so confused, Avery. So scared for you."

"I think part of me assumed I was dreaming, seeing her like that, following her through the wet grass. It felt like a dream. At least until I woke up in a padded cell."

"That's terrifying."

"Yes," she says soberly. "Are you still in Tanglewood? We're going there tomorrow. I want to see you."

"Actually we're on our way to the asylum."

"What? No. Turn around."

"I'm not sure the pilot can turn around in midair." I glance at Damon, whose expression has turned hard. "And I'm not sure we'd tell him to if we could. I think Damon needs to finish this."

A deep breath comes over the line. "Maybe that's true. I don't trust the FBI any more than I trust the people who ran that asylum. That man has some kind of hold over people. He gets into their heads."

I'm familiar with that particular sensation. The sense that he can see inside me. The feeling of invisible fingers combing through my worries and fears.

"That doesn't mean you need to go," she adds. "You shouldn't be anywhere near that place. Jonathan Scott is still there and very much alive. And he has the other inmates with him."

Nothing about padded walls and creepy asylums appeals to me. That would always be true, but doubly so because that's where Jonathan Scott hurt me three years ago, in an old abandoned mental hospital in the city. He feels at home there, which makes them the worst possible place to keep him. Where he's strongest.

"No," I say softly, because I have no intention of leaving Damon's side. "I'm going."

"Penny, no. You can't."

"I need to see this through. We all have our strengths, Avery. Yours got you out of that place. And mine... well, mine sent me there. That's the difference between us."

CHAPTER TWENTY-FIVE

WE LAND ON a private airstrip amid Cessnas and small luxury jets, the sunset casting an orange glow.

Whatever recreational use this place normally has, it's now been commandeered by Damon Scott. Five men in black T-shirts and military cargo pants wait for us with an arsenal that could rival a small nation. Large black guns lined up on white folding tables. They make me feel both better and worse—better, because we're more prepared for whatever might greet us at the asylum. And worse, because it brings home how dangerous it's really going to be.

Damon confers with the men in hushed tones, leaving me out of the discussion. I might take offense to that, but these men are clearly well-trained. I have no knowledge of combat. And I can't contain my relief that he isn't really going to *COME ALONE*, no matter what the note said.

Hiro finds me looking at an array of strange

little capsules. "Smoke bombs," she says.

I glance back at her. "Did you read about them in your magazine?"

"These? No, these are military grade. Classified. Not commercial."

"Then how do we have them?"

She only winks. "There are some good people here. I'm impressed, and I'm hard to impress. We'll set up camp for twenty-four hours. If Damon doesn't return by then—"

"What do you mean, if he doesn't return? I'm going with him." I say the words before I've had time to think it through, but it's true. The whole world turned their back on Damon Scott. All his life he's been suffering alone. This one time I can go with him.

"Not according to the plan."

"Screw the plan."

Her nose scrunches. "I'm not paid to run interference in a lover's spat."

Is that what we are—lovers? Friends? Enemies? Everything about Damon Scott is undefinable. He's a mystery that can't be solved. A puzzle with limitless layers. A living, breathing Escher painting with stairs folding into stairs for eternity. "This isn't a spat. This is important. We need to go with him."

"His orders are clear. He goes in alone."

Shock renders me speechless for a moment. "I hope that by alone you mean, with all these mercenaries, right? Because otherwise what's even the point of them?"

"Something else," she says, not sounding concerned. "If he doesn't return within twenty-four hours, you and I will board the plane and return to Tanglewood. The mercs have their own orders. I don't know the specifics, but I'm guessing they're going to turn the asylum into dust."

"With Damon inside?"

He appears behind me. "If I don't come out in twenty-four hours, I'm already dead."

I whirl to face him. "That is the worst plan I've ever heard."

A *tsk* sound. "And I worked so hard on it."

"I'm serious. How could you think that's a good idea?"

He puts a hand to his heart. "I'm wounded, sweet Penny. I don't have your brainpower, unfortunately, but I think it's a pretty good plan. You'll be safe with Hiro. The world will be safe from Jonathan Scott."

"You, Damon. You're the one who isn't safe."

"When have I ever been safe?" he asks, sounding infinitely weary.

The words hit me like a ton of bricks. He's never been safe. Not as a child. Not now. Does he even imagine it—or does it seem so far beyond his reach that it can't enter his dreams?

It only emboldens me to go with him. It will be like waking him from a nightmare, dangerous but entirely necessary to my soul. I can't watch him suffer alone.

"What did he do to you?" And this time I'm not asking about iron pokers or knives. I don't need to understand the details of his pain. I need to understand the goal.

"He made me into him," Damon says, more resigned than angry.

And that only strengthens my resolve to stay with him. I can't keep him safe against Jonathan Scott, but I can do something else. I can stand beside him. I can stand *in front* of him, protecting him the way he once protected me.

We sealed that deal with our bodies back in Tanglewood. The only reason he's standing here right now is because I begged him to. Because I took off my clothes. The last thing I'll do is make him face this alone, even if he thinks he has to.

"I'm coming," I say softly.

"No." His voice is firm, commanding. I'm

sure those paid mercenaries will jump to do his bidding, but they don't love him. *I love him.* I turn the words over in my head, wondering how it's possible. Wondering how I didn't see it for so long.

It's like saying *I love breathing.* Damon is part of the air itself.

"I'm coming with you, and you can't stop me."

He lifts a dark brow. "Do you really want to challenge me? I'll enjoy this. And what's more, I'll win."

Normally he might be right. This isn't normal. "I'm sure."

"Why do you even want to come? It's like walking into hell and asking for a cup of tea."

"Because I won't let you do that alone."

He looks away as if holding back words. "It's not up to you."

I run my hand along the outside of his arm. His body responds with a visible shiver. God, that makes me powerful. No one ever told me how much power's inherent to sex, how causing desire is addictive. Grasping his wrist, I tug him close.

"Let me come with you," I murmur, coaxing now.

"It's too dangerous."

"You'll be with me. I trust you to protect me."

His eyes meet mine, lids lowered. "You shouldn't."

"I've always trusted you. From the night you sat in my bedroom, reading the cover of my trigonometry book. I knew that I would be safe with you. And that's why I have to come."

His breath fans over my forehead as I lean close. "Why?"

"Because as long as you're with me, I'm safe. And as long as I'm with you, *you* are safe. It's only when we split up that he's been able to hurt us. Don't you see? He wants to divide us. This is how we stop him. This is how we survive. Together."

He curses and turns away, but he knows I'm right. That's the beautiful thing about logic, about proofs. The thing that's always drawn me to them, the way a well-reasoned argument becomes its own power.

"And if he hurts you?" Damon says, touching his forehead to mine.

"And if he hurts *you*?" I counter, because I would be just as devastated. More. Damon thinks that by heaping all the pain on himself, that he's keeping me safe, but the truth is I feel his scars like my own.

"Then it would be any other day."

I press my palm to his chest, where I know the darkened skin and white lines are not quite covered by tattoos of monsters and men. "That was before."

A hoarse laugh. "Was it? Feels about the same to me. The same as when I was a fucked-up kid with nowhere to go, knowing my dad was a fucking psycho."

"No, Damon Scott. It's different this time."

"Why's that?"

"Because this time you have me. And if I have to walk through hell to prove it, I will."

"Christ," he says.

The proof has already been solved. But I have another card to play. Something to gamble with. A clay chip with my own risk. "Please," I whisper.

You mean something to me, too. You mean everything.

His large body shudders. "What are you doing to me?"

Doing what I should have done all those years ago. "Thanking you. You protected me once. Let me return the favor. Let me help."

"No one else could come," Damon warns, his voice harsh.

I glance back at Hiro, who watches us solemnly. At the trained security men with their guns and muscles. And then at Damon, who looks at me with challenge. "Can you tell me why?"

"Because my father will kill them if they get close. They wouldn't even make it inside the door. And the death benefit clause in my contract with these guys is too expensive."

He keeps his voice light, but he cares about more than money. Otherwise he wouldn't be here.

"So if you don't come back, they would— what? Shoot from the outside?"

"Grenade launchers," he says as if he's discussing his poker strategy.

"Why don't you use them now?"

"The government frowns on private citizens destroying buildings," he says drily.

"That wouldn't stop you."

"It wouldn't," he agrees, speaking more slowly, more carefully. "What Avery did was incredibly brave. It was unbelievably strong. She got those nurses to safety, but…"

I search his eyes for some clue. "But what?"

"But the other inmates. They're still there. With him."

Oh God, the people who had been locked up. The ones who had helped Jonathan Scott. Should they be held accountable for their sins? For his?

It's one thing to decide that one man is beyond redemption, entirely another to condemn a whole asylum full of people to death.

CHAPTER TWENTY-SIX

DAMON DOESN'T EXACTLY agree I can come, but he does change his plans.

Instead of immediately making the two-hour drive from the small airstrip to the asylum, alone, he rides with our entourage to a small bed and breakfast, the kind with quilts thrown over the sofas and a long-haired cat staring at us moodily from the carpeted stairs.

An older woman greets us at the door, her smile fading when she takes us in.

Hiro steps forward. "We spoke on the phone a few minutes ago."

The woman attempts to recover, but she can't quite meet anyone's eyes. "Yes, of course. I'm so glad you called. We have three rooms available. I hope that will be all right."

"We'll make it work," Hiro says, her voice brusque.

"Thank you," I offer, knowing the woman is a little afraid. Her instincts are telling her that we're

188

dangerous, and she's right. We're just not dangerous to her.

She gives me a faint smile before bustling to an antique desk. "Here are the keys. The family suite has two rooms, one with a king-sized bed and the connecting room with two double beds."

Hiro accepts the keys with a nod. "The boys and I will take that one."

"And then there's the honeymoon suite. It's got a California king bed." She smiles in a motherly way. "We call it the Queen of Hearts room. You'll understand why when you see it."

Damon gives her his signature smile, which makes her blush. "I'm sure we'll love it."

The woman is still smiling when we head up the stairs. And immediately find out why the Honeymoon Suite is called the Queen of Hearts. Because there are hearts stitched into the bedspread. Painted on a canvas against the far wall. Hanging along the edge of the ceiling in little heart-shaped lights. I stare at the room from the open door, somewhat in shock.

From behind me Damon whistles. "Wow."

"It's absolutely insane."

"Don't tell me you're a cynic," Damon says, laughter in his voice.

Something brushes against my legs, and I look

down to see the cat winding its way in figure eights through Damon's legs, leaving white fur on black slacks. "Do you charm every female you meet?"

"Do you solve every math problem you see?"

"Yes."

I take a step into the room, wondering how I ended up sharing a bed with Damon Scott. There isn't a little servant's room available now. Maybe I can bunk with the woman who owns the place, wherever she sleeps. When we pulled into the gravel drive, there'd been nothing around for miles.

Damon follows me inside, nudging the cat out before closing the door, eliciting a plaintive meow.

"Where am I supposed to sleep?" I mutter, unable to look at him directly.

He laughs softly. "Are you afraid of me, sweetheart?"

"No." The tremble in my chest calls me a liar.

His body covers my back. His mouth lowers to my ear. "Are you shy? Did you forget what we did? Did you forget that I tasted your pretty pink cunt, that I licked you until you came all over my face?"

My cheeks must be on fire. That's how they

feel. "I didn't forget," I say, my voice high-pitched.

"Don't worry," he says, his mouth brushing the side of my neck. "I have no plans to touch you tonight. So you can stop shaking. In fact I'm going downstairs."

"Oh," I say, feeling faint. Disappointment knots itself in my stomach. It's more than disappointment. I want him to touch me again. He's become my addiction, more intensely and more dangerously than numbers ever have been.

"Go to sleep. Get some rest. You're going to need it."

I turn to face him. "You aren't going to leave tonight, are you? Promise me."

He flashes a quick smile. "Would you believe a promise from me? I'm a notorious liar. A criminal. I'm not a good person, sweetheart. You know that best of all."

"I believe you," I say solemnly.

He looks away, studying a clock shaped like a heart on the mantel. "I don't know why I'm even considering letting you come with me."

In some ways it might be crazy that I want to come, but it feels right. Deep in my bones, it feels more than right. It feels necessary. "Because you believe in me," I say softly.

"Of course I do," he says sadly. "It's not you that's the problem. It never has been. My father likes tests. He likes mind games. He likes moving people around on his own personal chessboard."

I try to make my voice light. "So you should definitely bring me. I love tests."

Dark eyes flash. "And if we get slowed down, if we fail, those soldiers are going to blast the asylum into a pile of rubble. With both of us inside. Understand? They're the failsafe. I can't risk him escaping. That's the one variable that can't change."

"Then we'll have to be quick."

"God," he mutters. "You drive me insane."

The word rings in the air, heavy now that we're faced with going to an actual asylum. That's where Jonathan Scott was tortured as a child, part of what made him twisted. Or would he have turned out that way no matter what? He tried to make his son a monster, but he failed. No matter what Damon Scott believes about himself, he's a good man.

I take a step closer to him. "Then punish me," I whisper.

Except I know he won't. He flinches away from the words, which only proves how much he wants that. Dominance and desire vibrate from him, almost tangible in the air. Did that come from his dark past or would Damon have been this way no matter what? People aren't equations. I thought I was the one who misunderstood, but it's Damon who thinks people are the sum of their past.

"Go to bed," he says, his voice harsh.

"Come with me," I counter, my chin high. Inside I'm terrified, but I know better than to let him see that. "You don't need to go downstairs. You only wanted to get away from me."

He makes a growling sound. "Don't test me."

"That's exactly what I'm doing," I say softly, because I'm tired of watching Damon deny himself.

Reaching for the hem of my shirt, I pull it over my head. My jeans come off next. And the entire time I'm undressing my gaze doesn't leave his, trying to convey both threat and warning. Trying to convey the same malice he sends me. I'm going to make him feel good, feel safe, for once in his godforsaken life.

He swallows hard. "Stop. Don't."

I have to smile, because even his protests feel half-hearted. The way he's looking at my body... I know he wants me. He more than wants me. He's dying for me, eating me up with his eyes.

When his lips part, I know he's remembering licking me, thinking he's going to do it again.

Instead I drop to my knees on the hardwood floor, looking up at him in only my bra and my panties. It took heavy courage to get to this point, so maybe that's why I'm suddenly feeling weak. "You can tell me if I'm doing it wrong."

"Christ," he mutters. "You don't want to do this. Not for me. Not for any man."

"Why not?" I ask, working the placket of his slacks. Already he's hard beneath my touch. The backs of my fingers brush his rigid length as I pull down the zipper, making it flex inside.

He speaks between gritted teeth, as if I'm hurting him—and maybe I am. He's so twisted up, as if pain is pleasure and pleasure is pain. "Because we're selfish. We'll use you and hurt you and get so deep inside you just so we can feel good."

I don't know if he's talking about me or him. My darker suspicion is that he's talking about his father.

With his slacks open, there's only black briefs cupping his erection. I run my palm over the warm cotton. He sucks in a breath. There's a sense of power as I stroke him through the fabric. A sense of pride as I make him buck into my hand.

"Don't deserve it," he gasps as I mouth him through the briefs. "We don't fucking—God, sweetheart. I don't fucking deserve you, and I definitely don't deserve *this*."

He pushes back against the closed door, slamming his fists against it, making the whole wall shudder. It's a denial, but not for me. For himself. He looks like some kind of dream, his head thrown back, his slacks open to reveal a thick erection. He would be the very picture of masculine sexuality except I don't think most men are so tormented about it. I don't think most men fight themselves.

I curl my fingers into the waistband of his briefs, tugging downward. His cock springs forward, even larger once it's released from its confines. My throat feels thick at the sight of it. The dark head and the smeared wetness at the tip. The vein running along the smooth length.

The scent of him makes me lightheaded—salt and faint sweat. I turn liquid inside. For once my mind falls silent from its calculations and its worry. There's only his maleness, his beautiful selfishness.

There's only making him feel good.

Grasping him at the base, I tilt his cock toward me. And press a single kiss to the tip.

He makes a startled sound, like he didn't expect this. Couldn't have predicted this. And maybe that's true. He's pushed me away so hard and so often that maybe I should have gone. Except for the way his hips push out, reaching for my mouth even as his back presses against the door.

"Tell me if I'm doing it wrong," I whisper again.

His breath shifts. "I'm going to hurt you, sweetheart. Don't let me hurt you."

But it doesn't hurt to slick my tongue over the tip. It doesn't hurt to wrap my mouth around the thick knob of him, to stretch my jaw to take him deeper. It isn't quite pleasure either, nothing like when he forced my thighs apart and made me cry out. This is something different, the act of service, the feeling of surrender as I use my body to please his. *Selfish, selfish,* and how is that a good thing? How is that sexy and alluring? I don't know the math behind it, but that's okay. My body understands. It makes me warm and hot at my core. It makes me clench my thighs in helpless anticipation.

I take him into my mouth again and again, using the same rhythm he used on me, feeling it in every throb of my body. A small spurt of saltiness appears on my tongue, slicking the way as he pushes in deeper. "Fuck," he says. "No. I can't. I shouldn't."

It suddenly seems like the worst kind of tragedy. Not even every scar on his body, as terrible as they are. It's *this,* the way he can't let himself feel pleasure. The way he can't even undress in a room full of undulating bodies, the way he can't let one of them touch him.

A sense of urgency overcomes me, and I put my other fist on his cock. They're both there, holding the part of him that's too far down for me to reach with my mouth. Even with both hands around him, there's enough of his cock to fill my mouth. To bump gently against the back of my throat.

My throat convulses, and the sound of my gag fills the room. My eyes water. Humiliation sweeps up my chest, for not being able to do this right, for being so bad at it, but he makes a helpless groan.

He wants that, I realize with a soft exhalation. Those fists against the door. They aren't about protecting himself from pleasure. They're about protecting me from pain.

Don't let me hurt you.

I lean back until he's not in my mouth, until my lips rest against the silk-smooth tip. And then my hands fall to my side, loose and defenseless.

"Hurt me," I whisper.

He stares down at me, struggling with himself. With his impulses. His past.

And then he grabs me in a sudden, terrifying rush. He turns me so that it's my back against the door. My fists against the wood. Somehow I keep from pushing him away from me, even when he presses his cock to my lips. He probably expects me to do that. He probably would stop if I did.

Instead I open to him, letting him press into my mouth harder and faster and deeper than I ever would have done it myself. He goes far enough that I'm gagging on the very first thrust, the back of my head knocking gently against the door.

One of his hands cups my jaw, holding me steady so that he can pull out and push back in.

There's no exploration like before, not tasting him or feeling him with my tongue. It happens too fast for that, too forcefully. I can only stare up at him with wide eyes, struggling to breathe.

"Is this what you wanted?" he says, sounding breathless. Sounding angry. "You wanted me to push my cock between your gorgeous, fuckable lips? You want me to make you choke?"

My eyes widen, but there's no time to protest. No time to do anything but suck in a breath as he pushes in deep enough that it feels like he's splitting open my throat, stretching tender flesh beyond its boundaries. Blocking the only path to air. My lungs burn, but nothing happens until he decides to pull out again. I'm completely at his mercy.

When he pushes back inside, I brace himself for another hard invasion.

Instead he holds himself in my mouth, enough to make me feel full but still with room to breathe. Still able to move my tongue. And that's what I do, flicking lightly along the ridge I can feel.

He swears softly. "That's beautiful. I'm going to take you deeper. Do you think you can take it?"

Deeper? God, I don't know if I can. The question is a course of electricity through my body. And the answer has to be yes. However it will fit. However it will feel—*yes.*

All I can do is nod, my lips still stretched around him.

He nods, his eyes intense, a dark sky with flashing lightning. He pushes in again, slowly, inexorably. Breaching a barrier I didn't know existed. My body revolts against the intrusion, bucking on its own. It doesn't make him flinch, my fight. He expected it. He accepts it, keeping his cock in my throat even as I convulse around him, reflexes trying to push him out.

My hands are up around my head, pressing back against the door in tight fists. Slowly I unclench them. Even with Damon's cock in my throat, I make my body relax.

"That's right," he murmurs. "So beautiful like that. So beautiful, and you're mine."

He grasps the base of his cock as he pulls away. With the heavy tip resting on my tongue, he strokes himself hard and fast. Once. Twice. And then he comes in large pulses, thick salt pushing against the back of my tongue, so intense it makes my eyes water. I swallow again and again, but there's still more of him. The taste of him so deep inside me I'll never forget it.

I pant against the door as he pulls away and zips back up. I half expect him to walk away from me. To gently set me aside so he can leave like he wanted to do.

Instead he crouches in front of me, his eyes knowing and sympathetic. He slips two fingers into my panties, reaching down until he finds the wet core of me. "You're hurting, aren't you?"

And it's true, I am. He said he would hurt me. My ache is sharp and relentless, only heightened by the calloused fingertips he rubs against my clit.

"Too much," I say, my hips rocking to get away, to get closer.

He silences me with a kiss, sliding his tongue against mine. He must taste himself in my mouth. I can only taste him as he devours me. As he thrusts two fingers inside me and rubs his thumb against my clit, hard enough that it hurts—and still I don't want him to stop.

There are starbursts in my eyes as he pushes me over the edge. I gasp into his mouth, hoping he can understand the message of my body—the need and the relief. His touch carries me through a long and airless orgasm as he murmurs, "I know. I'm sorry. It's over now."

Chapter Twenty-Seven

WHEN I STEP out of the bed and breakfast, Damon is leaning against one of the black SUVs. There's something incongruous about the sharp cut of his suit and the wide-open sky. About the shiny glint of metal set against a brownish rural expanse.

His expression doesn't change as I come outside and approach him.

I'm wearing one of my old well-washed pair of jeans and a Smith College shirt this morning. I wish I had cargo pants like the mercenaries. Or at least fuck-you boots like Hiro wears. Instead I've got faded sneakers that are coming apart at the seams.

"You waited for me," I say, unable to hide my surprise.

Without answering he steps away from the vehicle and holds the door open.

I climb into the passenger seat, marveling at the chivalry. It's a far cry from mocking me from the throne of a sex party. Then again maybe it's not so different. Damon has always been a rare combination of refined depravity.

He sits in the driver seat, pulling out of the dirt driveway in a smooth motion. I realize with a start that I've never seen him drive. Partly that's because I've gone to see him at the Den. Even when we leave Damon has drivers. He has security. He has house cleaners and staff, the way only rich people do.

No cook, though. That part he does himself, and I very much missed his cooking as I ate the oversweet muffins and stale coffee served in the floral dining room this morning.

"How long is the drive?" I ask as the road levels out to a single lane each way.

"Two hours and twelve minutes."

That's very exact. "Have you been here before?"

"No, but I've seen the schematics."

"Oh. Can I see them?"

He gives me a sideways look. "They're in the back."

I rummage through a black duffel bag before finding a roll of yellow paper with thick and thin lines. *Wharton County Prison.* My throat tightens. "I thought you said this was an asylum."

"It was decommissioned as a prison a long time ago. A private medical firm converted it to a mental institution for high-risk patients about five years ago."

The schematics show a large decagon, a shape with ten sides, built into a forest. The closest thing for miles is a small national park. I wonder how many hikers know what's nearby? Cells are marked off along each side of the polygon. At the center there's a hexagonal room marked *Security Headquarters.*

"Why was it decommissioned?" I ask, wondering if anyone ever escaped.

"The Quakers designed the prison to punish its inmates, basically creating solitary confinement for each of them. Unfortunately their idea of religious penance literally made men crazy."

I suck in a breath, imagining staring at the wall every single day. Alone. "Did they renovate it when they turned it into a mental institute?"

"Possibly, but this is the last floor plan we can find."

Indignance rises in my throat. "It was considered too cruel and unusual for criminals. How could they keep *patients* here? This is supposed to be a place that helps people."

Agitation becomes a physical thing, my heart

jolting and batting against my ribcage, nerves pinging around inside me. Hearing about this hospital only makes it worse. Only makes it *real.*

His profile looks severe. "Private institutions aren't subject to the same oversight that government-run prisons have. And with the amount of money this place charges, people aren't likely to complain."

My eyebrows press together. "What does that have to do with it?

He glances at me, dark humor lighting his black eyes. "Do you think celebrities don't have a crazy uncle? Or that the top politicians never had anyone in their bloodline go insane? These people need to disappear. And death—well, that's far too public."

Shock washes over me like ice water. "You're saying these people are being held against their will."

"Aren't all permanent residents of a mental hospital there against their will?"

"This is different."

"I'm not sure whether these people are a danger to themselves or to society. I'm not sure whether they'd walk out the door if it wasn't locked. What I do know is that Gabriel Miller paid a great deal of money with the assurance that my father would never have access to personnel."

"So what happened?"

"What happened is that it's impossible to guarantee that. Someone has to bring food. Someone has to administer medicine and clean his cell." His voice turns bitter. "And there are other inmates. Someone who thinks she's just like him, someone who has no idea she's a mouse living in a lion's den."

"Maybe she did know," I say softly. "Maybe she didn't have a choice."

The way I didn't have a choice when I worked at the diner for pennies. When I was forced to bring Jonathan Scott a piece of pie, even knowing that I was serving a predator.

"A lot of good that did her," Damon mutters.

I stare at him, realizing he's talking about someone specific. "Did you know one of the inmates?"

He glances at me, eyes widening in a brief and unlikely moment of shock. Then he turns back to the road, the moment over—or maybe it never happened. "Not here."

A wooden sign battered by decades of storms and neglect. Weeds coming up around it. I can see the picture clearly in my mind, the place where Jonathan Scott took me.

The place where his son rescued me.

"Tanglewood Mental Hospital," I say, a chill running through me.

"Yes." The word is hard. Almost a physical blow.

The more he pushes me away, the more I'm sure that he's where I need to go. That night is a blur to me, which is a small relief. I remember some parts clearly. I remember Jonathan telling me that he raised Damon in that terrible building, abandoned and dark and littered with torture devices they once thought might actually help.

Had Damon had a friend there? Had there been some young nurse that he was friends with? The thoughts send a course of jealousy through me, which is wrong for so many reasons. Not the least of which Damon is almost ten years older than me. He would have naturally been with another woman before I was even an appropriate age for him.

And wrong because I have no claim on this man. If he was able to find any solace in a horrifying situation, that's a good thing.

He shakes his head once, sharp. "There was no one."

The words strike me in the soft flesh of my heart. *No one.* "Then who—"

"My mother."

A knot forms in my throat. "You never told me about her."

"I never tell anyone about her."

I reach across the console for his hand and squeeze. I'm convinced he's going to pull away. Probably send me a scathing look for daring to touch him without permission, but he does something I don't expect. He squeezes back.

"She had schizophrenia," he says softly. "At least that's my best guess according to the records from the doctors. They had no idea what to do with her at the time. Mostly they just locked her up and tried every kind of barbaric treatment they could come up with."

"I'm so sorry," I whisper.

"Sometimes I think, can you even blame her for falling for Jonathan Scott? Her family had abandoned her. The doctors basically tortured her. He would have been the only man to show her any kindness."

"God. I'm sorry."

"And other times I think, maybe my father actually loved her back. They were both fucked up, both trapped. The asylum didn't want it known that they had let a patient get pregnant, especially one who was sixteen, so they kept it quiet. Had them married in secret as if that could erase the fact that she couldn't consent."

"How old was your father?"

"Twenty five."

About the same age difference between Damon and me. What a sad way for him to come into the world. My eyebrows press together. "Then what happened to you?"

"I stayed there," he says simply.

"A child. In an asylum. With actual patients."

He flashes me that signature smile, and I realize how much pain it hides. "Not exactly an idyllic childhood. They didn't actually treat me that badly, even though I think all the doctors assumed I would be batshit insane."

"That's terrible," I whisper.

God, no wonder he wouldn't send anyone else into the asylum to die there. And no wonder he wouldn't agree to blasting it to pieces, with the innocent patients inside. Patients like his mother. The only option was for him to come himself.

"I don't have very many memories. Running down the hallway. Sleeping in the same room as my mother. She would sing songs at night, but during the day her condition got worse. She wouldn't stop screaming. Wouldn't stop fighting."

We pull onto a paved road. A sign that's clearly new and crisp proclaims that this is private property, no trespassers, violators will be prosecuted. We must be close. "What happened?"

"They tried this new treatment. All of the inmates got daily exercise in the pool. They thought her wildness was a choice, that they could punish her out of it." He gives a laugh hoarse with grief. "They would hold her under longer and longer. Until she finally drowned."

My eyes close in pain, but not before I see the trees lined up in a neat row on either side of the road. We're about to go inside a building almost everyone would try to escape. And our only goal is to kill someone. Not just someone. One person in particular.

"That's when my father really snapped. News of her death came out in the press, and the place was shut down. Maybe we could have had a normal life, but he completely lost it after that. He believed that everyone was out to get him. That we would only survive by fighting, by stealing. By killing. And the worst part is, I understood. Even that young I knew that my mother was gone, and I knew exactly why. God, I understood him back then. What's sick is I understand it now."

CHAPTER TWENTY-EIGHT

THE FRONT OF the building looks brand-new, a smooth white exterior that might have been built five years ago instead of a hundred. Maybe they tore out the entire prison and made something new. That's my fervent hope as we speed along the smooth pavement.

Damon parks without any sense of fear or subterfuge.

I squint at the dark glass, where I can only barely make out a wide reception desk. "You aren't worried he's going to... shoot at us?"

Though even as I say the words, that doesn't feel like Jonathan Scott's style. There are many terrible words I could use to describe him. Monster. Sadist. But he isn't a coward.

"Why would he do that? He could have come to Tanglewood if he wanted me dead."

I glance at him, taken aback by how casually he discusses his death. "So he isn't going to hurt you?"

His laugh is a cold sound. "Oh, he'll hurt me. Pain only makes you stronger, don't you know? But he won't kill me. Not yet. He would have stopped anyone else from entering these doors, though. That's why I couldn't have brought the mercs, even if I wanted to."

My footsteps falter. *COME ALONE.* "Will he stop me from entering?"

"No."

"How do you know?"

"Because I do." Damon looks back at me, and his eyes soften. "I can't swear to you that you'll be safe here. I want you on the other side of the country. I want you on the other side of the world. On the moon. But I will do everything in my power to let you walk out of here unharmed."

It comes to me as I watch him in the over-bright sun, standing in front of a modern asylum, that all he knows is sacrifice. All he knows is running through the halls of a dangerous mental hospital or leaving people behind so they don't get hurt. Even coming here is a form of sacrifice, searching for some way to save the inmates who are still here and still alive.

Of course Damon doesn't want *me* here, where I might get hurt, in defiance of every sacrifice he's ever made, and it's a testament to his respect for me that he's even honoring my request to come.

"I trust you," I say softly.

I'm the one who pushes the door open, who steps inside first. He strides in after me, immediately moving to block my body with his. This is how it will be, unless I stop him. With him throwing his body in front of mine. He can't stop himself. I'm the one who has to stop him.

"Lovely," he mutters.

The place is eerily empty, the front desk unmanned, security stations to the right and left unguarded. There's a cup of coffee in the waiting area, sitting cold and full beside one of the chairs, as if someone just got up to go to the bathroom and disappeared. It feels like waking up in Avery's room, but she's missing. Everyone is missing.

"We should go to the security headquarters," I say.

He glances at me, curious. "I have his room number from Gabriel."

It was clear the second I looked at the schematics. How anyone in the outer circle, kept apart, would yearn to be in the center. It would literally make someone insane to sit at the outer edges. They wouldn't stay there if they had the run of the place.

"He'll be in the center."

Damon looks like he considers arguing. And then he nods, once. And that trust takes my breath away. We move in long purposeful strides, directly back into the heart of this dark building. How many people went crazy between these walls? Some were already crazy, but others— others became that way.

Around a corner I come to a halt. There are bodies strewn along the ground, dressed in beige, covered in blood. Oh God. Are these the nurses taken hostage? The other patients he couldn't control?

Damon steps around their bodies with casual indifference.

As I follow behind him I realize they're local police. This is what authorities sent in to deal with the situation? More death, more suffering. And for nothing.

We come to another set of glass doors, this one completely blackened with some kind of tinting. There's writing on the glass. Numbers and symbols scribbled in permanent marker. It's a proof, I can see that right away. The kind I would love to mull over with a cold cup of coffee.

And the marker sits on the floor directly in front.

"One of his fucking tests," Damon mutters.

"Then let's pass it." I'm not going to waste time. There's a clock counting down our lives. I lean down to pick up the marker, but Damon grabs it first.

"Tell me what to write and I'll do it."

"That's not how it works. I need to think it through while I solve it." I reach for the marker, but he holds it up high, like a high-stakes game of monkey-in-the-middle.

"No."

I glare at him. "Why not?"

"Because it's probably rigged," he shouts.

Realization sinks into my stomach, cold and heavy. This glass is probably only tinted one way. The person on the other side of the door can see us. Or maybe they're just using cameras. Jonathan Scott is still controlling things from behind the curtain.

"I know you want to protect me," I say softly. "But this proof? He left it for me. That means I need to solve it. This is why I had to come, even if I didn't know it."

A muscle ticks in Damon's jaw. He doesn't want to let me. He doesn't even want me to be here, but I'm as much a part of this as he is. Maybe he does see that, because he holds out the marker.

It takes me longer to do the proof because it's in a domain I haven't worked in lately—trigonometry. I draw angles and equivalencies beside the door to remind myself of them. Then I solve the proof directly on the door, working line by line.

The strange thing about the proof is that, despite its complexity it's not meaningful or even very interesting. Almost as if it's making me think in circles for no reason.

Only when I get to the end do I realize what he's done.

Sigma for the sum of a sequence.

Psi, the closest greek alphabet letter to W.

Epsilon, epsilon, theta.

He's spelled out SWEET PEACH, which is what he called me when he hurt me.

Damon swears under his breath. The doors open with a muffled whoosh, and from instinct I jump back. He moves in front of me, but there's no one on the other side. They must be mechanized. Someone controls them, a puppetmaster— so what does that make me?

My sneakers crunch on glass as we step inside. I look up to see a modern glass light, only half of it remaining in a long jagged edge. It suddenly seems silly to have such an impractical fixture in such an important place. Why are the walls in such a secure place made of glass?

They probably never expected inmates to break out of their cells. They never expected Jonathan Scott. Like the *Titanic* that couldn't sink, they were brought down by their own hubris.

Only once we're inside do I see the man sitting behind the wall of monitors.

Jonathan Scott is such an intimidating presence that it's strange to see him wearing plain white scrubs and a five-day-old beard. He looks unkempt and tired, as if years of terrorizing people have caught up to him. Only his eyes look the same as I remember them, silver and sharp, as when he came to me on the elementary school playground.

"Hello, Son," he says in that silky, scary voice of his.

Damon doesn't crack a smile. That signature charm that he can give out evaporates completely, leaving only a cold stone of a man. "You summoned. So here I am."

"You say that as if I should have expected it. But you were never very obedient."

"No, but you figured out how to get me here

anyway."

"It's a father's prerogative, wouldn't you say?"

That prerogative is plainly visible in the wall of flat screens behind Jonathan Scott, the video cameras pointing into each cell. Some of the inmates pace in their cells. Others lie on their beds.

And still others are twisted at odd angles on the floor. Already dead.

"I thought they were working for you," I say, my voice hoarse. "They helped you take the nurses captive. Helped you keep them prisoner. Why are they locked up?"

"They failed," Jonathan says sharply, his eyes flashing with venom.

They failed because Avery helped the nurses escape.

She was kept in this asylum for hours, for days. And now I'm here, a mental hospital like the one where I was attacked, a place completely different from that abandoned building. That had been moss-covered and dirt-blackened. This place is sterile and cold. The only thing they have in common is the callousness of the people who ran them.

"Spare us the sob story," Damon says, his voice cold. "You are a kind and benevolent leader.

Someone dared to disobey you. And now you have to kill and torture people to make things right."

Jonathan's smile reveals teeth stained with blood. My chest constricts. How would his mouth be bloody? Is he injured? He sits in a casual and comfortable way. Then again he would be excellent at hiding pain.

A darker thought occurs to me. What if he put that blood there—by drinking it? By biting someone, so deep and so intensely that their blood spilled into his mouth?

My stomach turns over, and I press my hands to it, grateful I didn't finish that muffin this morning.

"Do I disgust you, sweet peach?" Jonathan Scott says in a singsong voice.

"Don't speak to her."

"Then why did you bring her if she isn't going to play?"

"I brought her because you preyed on her when she was only a child. And I know from experience how large you can loom in memory. But you aren't that grand, really. You aren't as scary or as smart as you think you are. And who better to see you for who you really are than Penny?"

Jonathan's face lights up with twisted pleasure. "She is a smart girl. Outsmarted me when she was barely a baby, didn't she? Skinny legs and pigtail braids, and there she was pretending to be dumb so I wouldn't take her. Thinking about it is enough to make me hard."

Damon pulls out a gun so quickly and so smoothly I barely have time to register the sharp turn in conversation. "And now she gets to see you die, you sick fuck."

No surprise registers on Jonathan's face. No fear, either. "I won't deny you your chance to kill me, my boy. But you know it will mean I'll have won. That I've finally turned you into me."

"Maybe so, but I won't mourn you for even a second."

Another sly smile. This one raises the hair on the back of my neck. "But I think I'll take something with me when I go. You'll mourn her, won't you?"

My heart skips a beat because I know exactly who he's threatening. Me.

Damon knows too. His head whips toward me, his eyes frantic as he makes sure that I'm standing, still safe. And it's that split second of distraction that Jonathan uses to lunge at him. With almost superhuman speed he crosses the yards between them, pushing Damon's gun wide. A shot blasts through the air, crumpling drywall in the corner of the room.

Jonathan tackles his son to the ground, ripping the gun from his hand.

Pure instinct sends me reeling back, out of the path of men and guns. Not fast enough, because Jonathan moves toward me in a blur of feral silver eyes. Then I'm on the ground, a gun pressed to my temple, a heavy weight on top of me, shards of glass pressing into my back in starbursts of pain.

A metallic scent enters my lungs, and I realize it's the breath of Jonathan Scott. As if he's been more than bleeding. As if he's *breathing* blood somehow. I gag against the smell of decay.

The whispery laugh sends a chill down my spine. "Now what are you going to do?" Jonathan asks. "Are you going to shoot me? Are you going to risk my finger slipping on this trigger?"

My head turns to the side, half an inch, and I can see Damon has produced another gun. He must have had several weapons on his body. His face is a mask of cold determination as he points it at his father.

"Let her go," he says, his voice betraying no fear.

Nothing about him says that he's afraid for

me, nothing except his hesitation. And his father knows it too, because he sounds almost gleeful. "This is what has made you weak, Son. This is what I've been trying to stamp out of you, and today I'll finally do it. You'll have to kill her to kill me."

"No," I whisper against his sacrifice. "Damon. Shoot him."

A pause. "Don't move, Penny."

He won't do it. He won't risk me, which is what Jonathan Scott calls his weakness. But I know better. It's his strength. The thing that says he's still human, despite an upbringing of horror and pain. Despite every single card stacked against him, he's human.

Without moving my body, without averting my gaze, I trail my left hand along the floor. Along the bed of glass that I'm lying in. And find a single shard long enough to pierce.

"Damon," I whisper.

"I'll get you out of this," he promises, but there's desperation in his voice.

A deep well of sadness runs through me. "No, you won't."

And he shouldn't have to. This isn't his battle. It's mine.

With a strength I find deep inside me, I ram

the shard of glass into Jonathan Scott's neck. Even knowing that he might pull the trigger in that split second. That his spasming body might pull the trigger and kill me as it goes.

It takes more force than I could have anticipated. The throat seems like a vulnerable place, but there's flesh and tendons and cartilage. It violates every tenet of my humanity to do this— this act that Jonathan has been trying to force from his son for years.

The glass cuts both ways, slicing my hand open even as it forges ahead.

But I was made for this. I have cold calculation instead of mercy. I have numbers, that tell me one death is far better than hundreds. I have the certainty, the logical proof written out inside my head, that tells me I need to be the one to kill Jonathan Scott—not Damon.

Even once the glass lodges itself completely into Jonathan's throat, he doesn't die. His silvery eyes stare down at me, still seeing, still alive. In them I see both shock and gratitude, both fury and an overwhelming relief. This is an animal who needs to be put down.

It's the bullet in his head that sends him toppling off me.

The gun beside me blasts loud enough to

make my ears ring. It feels like the pain, the *boom* of it, and I wonder inanely if I've been shot. Then there are arms holding me, feeling me all over, checking me. Damon can't seem to stop running his hands over me, assuring himself I'm alive.

I can't hear anything, the sound of the shot loud enough to take away my hearing, but I can see Damon Scott's lips moving. And I recognize the words, in that soul-deep way, because I feel them too. *I love you, I love you, I love you.*

CHAPTER TWENTY-NINE

IT TAKES TWENTY-FOUR hours for my hearing to return, but in that time a lot changes.

Damon makes the drive back to the bed-and-breakfast, on the phone most of the way. I watch his lips part of the time as he speaks to Hiro in brusque sentences about bringing in the FBI. A few minutes in I fall asleep, the shock and adrenaline overloading my system.

When I wake up again, I'm covered in Damon's jacket, leaning against the window. The SUV has stopped in the same place it was parked last night, the sun shining. It's almost like the whole world *hasn't* shifted on its axis, but I know different.

There are five black and blue unmarked FBI sedans, two police cruisers, and an ambulance waiting in the dirt parking lot for us. Damon steers me to the ambulance and then disappears, leaving them to do tests on my hearing, tests for a concussion, a thorough physical documenting every cut from the glass, every dark bruise across my torso from the impact of Jonathan Scott pushing on top of me.

It takes hours for Damon to deal with the FBI, and once he does, we're on his private jet back to Tanglewood. I promptly fall asleep in the cushy leather seat, dozing for the entire three-hour flight.

By the time we reach the private airfield outside the city, I long for the cot in my small room. I long for the trays of delicious food that appear outside my door, the safety of knowing that Damon Scott protects me with more than just his money or his weapons—he guards me with his body.

But he doesn't take me to the Den.

We pull into the grounds I recognize as Gabriel Miller's mansion.

I think I've reached a state of numbness. The loss of hearing helps with that. Or makes it worse, depending on your perspective. I'm just fine not feeling anything.

I would put off feeling forever if I could.

Avery greets me at the door, tears darkening her hazel eyes. She pulls me close for a tight hug. The men are different from us, less emotional— on the outside. Less affectionate. But they still greet each other with what feels like both gratitude and apology, the source of their divide gone. The men disappear into Gabriel's study to talk.

I'm led to a comfortable sitting room with low couches covering most of the floor. Avery almost pulls me into her lap, clucking over my injuries and petting my hair. It feels strange to be fussed over. Even as a child when I got hurt, I found my own Band-Aids or went without.

And I can't deny that it feels *good* to be fussed over. To know someone cares.

I can only hear her intermittently, everything still muted. "I'm so proud of you," she says. "Damon told us what you did on the phone. How you were the one to bring him down."

Is that what happened? That isn't how I would have said it. It's Damon who brought us there, Damon who faced his own personal monster. And I helped. There *is* a kind of pride that I helped.

I mumbled answers to the paramedics, nodded or shook my head to Damon on the way here. Only now do I find my voice to speak, woman to woman. "The nurses?"

Her eyes turn cloudy. "They're okay. Some of them more than others."

"Where are they?"

"Most of them went home, if they had families to take care of them. The rest went to a women's shelter who will help them heal and start over."

I don't need to ask what Jonathan Scott did to them while he had the chance. I already know what he's capable of. My body remembers the violation of it intimately. "And you?"

She sighs. "I don't know. I want to say that I'm fine. Especially seeing what the other women had to endure, it feels wrong to complain."

"Your journey is your own," I whisper.

Her eyes meet mine, clear again. "Yes. My journey hasn't always been easy, but I have help. I have Gabriel, who hasn't left my side for a moment since it happened. And I have you."

I lean my head against her shoulder, trying to imbue her with strength. "What about you?" she asks softly. "Do you have someone?"

She isn't asking about someone, though. She's asking about Damon. And the truth is I don't know how to answer that. He loves me. He's said it, but the idea still seems far away. Detached. Maybe that's because I'm still processing what happened, but I think it might be him. That he loves me in that abstract, unobtainable way that says we'll never be together. That he can love me only from afar.

And that seems to be confirmed when Gabriel finds us an hour later, telling us that Damon has left, that he isn't coming back. That I'm free to stay there for as long as I need.

CHAPTER THIRTY

THE DEN SPILLS light and laughter onto the street. I step out of the cab knowing that I don't have much hope of doing anything here, but I couldn't bring myself to register for classes last week. Couldn't return to Smith without going to Damon one last time. Without fighting for us.

It's been two weeks since he left me at Gabriel Miller's sprawling modern castle.

Two weeks of wondering if he would come back for me. He didn't.

Two bouncers built like linebackers ignore me as I step inside the house. There isn't anyone having sex on the floor of the foyer, but I can see undulating bodies in the corner behind the stairs. Most people are dancing to a low and heavy beat. It's the perfect rhythm for pressing legs together, for pushing tongues against each other.

Everyone here ignores me as I squeeze past bare skin and leather and lace.

I'm wearing something a little party-ish tonight, a sapphire-blue dress that I borrowed from Avery. The satin fabric hugs my body. I can't help but feel exposed even with no one looking at me.

Damon ignores me as I wind through the crowd. He doesn't look up from his conversation even when I stand directly in front of him. But I feel his attention like a heat lamp, making me blush.

"Damon," I say.

A man wearing only sparkly leather pants kneels beside Damon's chair. His visible erection says he'd like to do a lot more than talk, but Damon reclines without any sense of urgency or interest. He has on slacks and a white dress shirt, rumpled but still dashing.

"Excuse me," I say louder.

A hush comes over the conversation around us. The man with leather pants stops talking. Only then does Damon lift his head, his black eyes meeting mine. A spark of anticipation heats my body from the center spreading out.

"What can I do for you?" he asks, his voice mocking.

God, I knew better than to come here. I did, but here I am anyway. "Can I speak to you in private?"

"Private," he says, considering. "What's the

fun of doing things in private? Anything you want to do in a room we can do out here. Isn't that right?"

The question is posed to the crowd, who laugh and tell him *yes, please, do.*

There won't be any emotion between us. No relationship. There's only *this,* mocking me in public, saving me in private, the hero who won't let himself be happy.

My throat burns. "Please don't do this."

He smirks. "I'm not doing anything yet. Would you like something? You look delicious in that dress. Like a cupcake. Very sweet. Should I lick you and find out if you are?"

There's a part of me so in love with this man that I want to say yes. So desperate for any part of him that I'll take this fake showman instead of the real person inside. "No."

"Or maybe you'd like to trade places. You could be queen of the Den, ruling from on high while I kneel in front of you." His smile is taunting. "I could kiss your feet. Would you like that?"

The people around me laugh, egging him on. They would watch him crawl for me, watch him debase himself with glee, but more than that, they want him to humiliate me.

"Higher and higher," he murmurs. "I could kiss your pretty pink…lips."

Of course he's not talking about my mouth.

He's talking about the place between my legs.

What would Damon do if I started undressing in front of everyone? If I accepted his challenge and displayed myself here? I think he would stop me, but that would mean admitting that I matter.

And anyway, that's not what I want to do. I don't want to force his hand. To challenge him into it. He doesn't want me, or maybe he doesn't want me *enough*.

I still can't help myself from asking one more time, from begging—even if that makes me a masochist. My love for this man ran so deep I almost didn't recognize it myself. It's like breathing or thinking. Like being. That won't stop if he makes fun of me, if he sends me away, but I don't want him to.

My pride is a physical lump in my throat. I have to swallow it, force it down so I can get the words out. "Damon Scott, I want you. I think you want me too. But I need you to say it. I need you to be with me." My voice cracks. "I can't stand here alone anymore."

It's all the courage I have in the world. All the dignity, which isn't much. I'm not the honorable

Avery James who can watch as the love of her life jets around the world in solitary danger.

I'm the girl from the slums of Tanglewood, the broke-down Cinderella who never got her prince.

The crowd watches me in breathless silence. Whatever happens next, I'm the best piece of entertainment they've seen in a while. Nakedness and sex are fine for depravity, but nothing compares to this—to baring my soul, my fears, my hopes to a man who doesn't want them.

Women look on with blatant jealousy. How much would they want Damon Scott kissing their feet?

His dark eyes are hooded, his mouth set in a hard line.

If his voice had been soft or hard, I could have had a chance. Instead it's jovial, more the showman than ever before. "If you want me, you can have me, sweet girl. Anything you want. Money. Sex. I'm yours to command."

My breath hitches. Money. Sex. He left out the things I want most. He wants to worship me in this pretend way, to make a show of it instead of something private.

"Fine," I tell him. "Then get on your knees."

It's like the room sucks in a breath. I can hear

them gasp, feel the shift in the air.

Damon's eyes turn sharp as a blade. He studies me for long seconds, looking at my challenge from every angle, but this is what he wants. This is what he asked for.

In a slow languid motion he moves to the floor in front of him, on his knees in his bespoke slacks, black hair in artful disarray, white dress shirt rumpled. He looks like a man well-sex and thoroughly debauched. The only thing he doesn't seem is submissive.

Like putting a wild jaguar on a leash. It's only a matter of time until I get bitten.

"What next?" he asks, his voice dangerously soft.

"Kiss my feet." I don't know why I'm pushing him, don't know what I hope to accomplish. Maybe that he'll give me real emotion instead of this fake sexed up version.

He bends down in a low mocking bow, all the way to the floor. The satin heels I'm wearing also came from Avery. They don't belong to me anymore than this dress. Anymore than this man. I don't feel victory as his lips touch my shoes. I'm too hollow for that, made of air and wanting. And a permanent desolation that this is all I'll ever be.

If this is all he can give me, why not take it?

"Higher," I tell him.

He narrows his eyes. "You want me to taste you in front of everyone?"

"No, you want that. Are you going to go back on your word?"

His smile is pure challenge. Then he ducks his head to my ankle, pressing a gentle kiss on the outside. Another on my knee, an almost innocent peck. Strange how even two inches above that point becomes indecent. And another two inches—obscene.

He ducks beneath the ruched hem, lifting it only enough to reach me. I'm mostly covered to the crowd who's avidly watching, some whispering behind their hands, others openly pointing. Even so it feels unbearably intimate as a mouth brushes over my panties.

Heat sparks in my sex from his soft kisses. Damon mocks me in front of a crowd, but underneath my dress he's pure tenderness. In the dark where no one can see, he's different. So gentle I almost can't feel him, but the building tension inside my body proves that I can. This is what we could have together.

"This is how it would be," I whisper as he caresses the backs of my thighs.

No one can hear me, though—not even him.

If this is all he can give me, why not take it? Because now I know the sweetness I'll never have, the love he can't give. Except it's more than ability. It's his choice. Even while he nuzzles against my mound, inhaling deeply, raising goosebumps on my skin, he's turning me away. By demanding that we do this here, now, instead of in private.

There's nothing here for me. Not safety. Love. *Damon.*

Those things aren't waiting for me at Smith College, either, but at least I don't have to see him like this. Mathematics is a poor substitute for human touch, I've learned. It's no longer the pinnacle for me. No longer the dream. Instead it's a consolation prize.

The solace I'll find after the quiet sorrow of Damon's refusal.

I take a step back, letting my dress unveil him, disheveled and lust-dazed.

"Very pretty," I tell him, my voice harder than I feel. "But it's not enough."

Even as I turn and walk out the door, I know that I won't ever stop hoping for him. Won't ever stop longing for the peace I found in his embrace. I used to think I understood numbers but not people, logic but not emotions. I know better now. We're really just equations longing for that other half of us. I can walk away from Damon Scott because he wants me to, but I can't stop loving him. It's part of who I am, the logic as simple and undeniably sad as that.

CHAPTER THIRTY-ONE

I WAKE UP in the middle of the night, back in my room in the Emerald. On the far corner I can see my desk made of textbooks and a chopping block. A poster for Smith College chess club on the wall.

For a moment I'm not sure why I woke up. Maybe because I know this will be my last night here. No more walking through manicured bushes and stately old buildings. No more small talk with trust fund babies. I came here for the mathematics, but more than that, I came here to escape. I still don't know where I belong, but I no longer need to run.

A shift in the air makes me hold my breath. I'm not alone in here. It's such a small room, the door locked. There's no way someone made it inside, especially without me noticing.

"Ramsey problems," comes a low and familiar voice.

My heart speeds up, a *thud thud thud* in my

ears. "What are you doing here?"

"You really think you can solve poverty like a word problem?"

When I sit up, I can see the large shadow sitting in the corner. He holds something in his hands. Not a textbook, but pieces of paper. "'As a first step in this direction, we develop a lower bound on elasticity,'" he says.

That's when I realize he's holding my research paper. "That's private."

"Is it, though? If it's going to be published in a professional journal? Congratulations, by the way."

The official name on the paper is Dr. Robert Stanhope, since no serious academic journal would consider publishing work by an under-graduate. I'm getting byline credit, which is still pretty cool.

"I don't know if I can solve poverty, but I'm going to try."

"You could try in Tanglewood. There's still plenty of slums and addiction plaguing the city."

I had planned to go to Tanglewood, but only in a loose and tenuous way. It will always be my home, the city of my heart, but I wasn't sure I could handle running into Damon Scott. Wasn't sure I could handle having him mock me just to prove he didn't care about anything or anyone.

It's been months since I last set foot there. Months since I walked out of the Den, my head held high, my heart in pieces. Now that I've graduated, I want to go back.

Bitterness seeps into my voice. "And sit in your lap? Have you kiss my feet?"

A rough sound. "I'm sorry about what I said."

"Sorry," I repeat dully.

"Sorry that I was a bastard. Sorry that I'm not worthy of you."

"Don't mock me," I say sharply. "Not here. Not now when there's only two of us."

"I'm not mocking you. I'm *not* worthy of you, Penny. Never have been."

"Then why are you sitting on the floor of my room, the same way you were when I was six years old."

"Because I'm the same person I was back then too—hungry and scared and so fucking lonely I would have done anything to be close to you."

Something fits into place in my heart, a proof that has an answer. I can't quite trust it, though. Logic only takes me so far. There's still enough hurt to cloud the answer. "And that makes me— what? The girl who found you by the lake? Someone who offers you a pillow?"

"Yeah," he says, his voice hoarse.

"What about your parties? I'm sure someone there would bring you to their bed."

"I don't want them. You know that. I never did." He sets the papers down beside him. Runs a hand through his hair, ruffling it in that way that makes him not only handsome but devastating. "I never slept with anyone there."

"Never?" I ask, amused at the idea of Damon Scott as a monk.

"I lost my virginity when I was eight," he says, and my amusement turns to dust. "I've slept with a lot of people in my life. Some by choice. Some not. But when you were sixteen, I kissed you."

My breath catches, because I remember that kiss. I can't forget that damned kiss.

"I haven't touched anyone since."

"God, Damon. Why are you telling me this?"

"You know. Do you want me to beg? I deserve that. And I'll do it."

I make a sound of fierce denial. "Stop."

"I'm not mocking you." He laughs, self-deprecating. "I wasn't mocking you then, not really. Do you know how I dream about you? About serving you? I'm always at your feet, Penny. Always beneath you."

"So you want to serve me? You want to obey

me?"

"Yes," he says, so fervently I almost believe him.

"Come here then."

It's hard to be this close to him and not curl into his chest. Hard to see him smile and wonder if it's real. It would be so easy to believe every word that comes out of his handsome mouth, but I've learned to be careful. If nothing else, dealing with Jonathan Scott has taught me that. With a dark sense of wonder I realize he's left that legacy.

Damon stands and crosses the room in two long strides. There's a man in my room. Not just any man, but one who owns a whole city. One who's done terrible things.

One who's saved my life.

It would be such a relief to say yes, to absolve him of everything. To hold him to my chest. To fall into his arms and let him take care of me, but I'm not that girl anymore.

"Beg," I say instead.

Damon Scott does not hesitate. He falls to his knees in front of my small bed, his head lowered. He's as much a supplicant now as he was a king before. "Let me touch you. Let me hold you. Let me love you the only way I know how."

There's a tremor in my chest, but it's been too

long. A semester since I left him. Weeks since he told me he loved me. Years since I first loved him. "What if it's not enough?"

His voice when he speaks holds a note of fervent prayer, as if I'm more than a person. "When you were small, I loved you as a child— smart and generous. When you were a teenager, I loved you as a young woman, strong enough to face anything."

I watch him, unable to look away, almost unable to breathe.

"When I saw you walk into the Den, I knew you were more than I could survive. You were the death of me. Every fake smile and stupid fucking laugh. Every time someone thought they were seeing the real Damon Scott. You broke every-thing."

"Do you want me to apologize?"

"I want you to come home," he says, looking up. The impact of his black gaze meeting mine makes me shiver. "I've dreamed about you, every night that you're not with me. I've wanted you for longer than is strictly legal. I *need* you beyond what I can endure. But that's not why you should go."

My voice is a whisper. "Why then?"

"Because you belong there. And if you do, I'll

spend every breath in my body protecting you, cherishing you, making sure you never need anything because you already have it."

I have to close my eyes against the wave of desire that hits me. The promise in his voice reverberates deep in my core. "Cherishing me. That makes it sound like I'm fragile."

"Not fragile," he says, low and deep. "Strong."

"Strong enough to handle what you gave me before." In the bed and against the door. "Strong enough to want you to do it again."

His large body jerks, as if the words are a physical blow. "Now?" he asks.

"Forever," I tell him, and he meets me at the end of the word with his lips to mine. His body pushing me back against the bed. His erection hard against the inside of my thigh.

He kisses me as if we've been apart for twenty years, like we might not see each other for another twenty. He kisses me as if we have every day for eternity, slow and deep and thorough. "I'll make it up to you," he murmurs between nips and licks as he kisses his way across my jaw and down my neck. "I swear I will."

"There's nothing to make up," I say on a gasp, arching my body upward.

"Everything," he says, tugging the shorts to

my pajama set down. "Everything, everything."

I grasp his hair, pulling him so he's forced to look at me. His eyes are hazy with lust. I clench my fist, the pain in his scalp enough to make him gasp. He focuses on me.

"Nothing to make up," I repeat. "This isn't an apology. I don't want that. This is every day. This is you and me. This is the way you love me and the way I love you back."

"God, yes," he mutters, and only when I release him does he lower his head.

He presses his face between my legs, breathing in as if surfacing after a long time underwater. His mouth makes open kisses on the inside of my thigh, moving closer and closer to the center before switching to the other side. When he reaches the center, he sighs—a sound so replete I feel it vibrate in my clit. He licks long and wide through my core, a languid move that makes me buck my hips.

"I love you," he whispers, and this time I hear him.

This time I can whisper it back. "I love you too."

He kisses me for agonizing minutes, endless hours. Until his lips are slick and his eyes dazed. When at last he enters me, I'm so swollen it feels like he barely fits. So tight that there's strain on his face as he pushes inside. Even with the slickness of my arousal it's hard to accept him. He rocks against me, slow and persistent.

Until finally my flesh spreads for him. I didn't save my virginity for him. I saved it for myself. To experience this with a man who loved me, who had the courage to prove it.

The way he thrusts inside me is both worship and possession.

A private altar at which he can pray.

He pushes inside me until I'm the one begging, incoherent, made supple by his tender assault, close enough to orgasm that it hurts. He doesn't speed up, no matter how much I urge him or rock my hips up. It's a steady march that he uses, bringing us both to the peak. Holding my wrists down on the bed when I want to touch him. Forcing himself inside me when it's too much. Going on forever even when I spasm and clench and cry out, breaking apart the way I broke him, becoming something new.

Epilogue

"**P**LAY WITH ME," Avery begs.

Gabriel demurs for about half a second before sitting down across from her. He couldn't deny her much before, but the larger her tummy grows, the more he anticipates her every whim. I think he'd build a castle on a cloud if she asks for it by the time we get to nine months.

A large crystal-cut chess set presides over the room, available for anyone to play. They begin their game, sparring with words as well as pieces.

The Den is still a private club in the city, but less about sex or gambling. Now it's a place where the citizens of Tanglewood can gather to discuss sex and mathematics, to eye fuck and play chess.

The city still has poverty and violence. There isn't an equation that fixes that, no matter how late I stay awake and work. But it has hope, too. I finally found Jessica and her baby, moved to a rural town outside the city. Brennan's going out with a schoolteacher at our old elementary school.

Even my father called last week to tell me he found a new place, that he would keep in touch as much as he could.

Damon appears at my side, his hand on my shoulder. "Need anything?" he asks.

"Only you."

He leans against the side of the chair, casual and alert. There's a peace he's found since Jonathan Scott died in that asylum, but he's still more wary than normal people. More dangerous and cunning and powerful than normal people. Normalcy is overrated, anyway.

There are a lot more chairs around than when he ran the place alone. All kinds of chairs—modern leather pieces with silver bases, old antiques with velour fabric, quirky armchairs with patchwork material. A place for everyone who wants a seat, but I have to say I'm partial to the chair that Damon Scott used as his throne. And when I sit here, Damon tends not to sit at all. Instead he stands beside me, both above me and below, owning me and owned.

And if we're alone, he'll kneel and use his mouth for something else.

"She's going to win," he comments, glancing at the chessboard.

"She usually does."

"Pretty sure Gabriel thinks she's going to leave him if he doesn't win some of the time."

I hide my smile. "Avery loves him. But she does like a challenge."

"As do you, sweet girl."

My eyes widen in pretend surprise. "Is that what you are? A challenge?"

He laughs softly. "Would you want me any other way?"

I take his hand in mine, squeezing gently. "Dangerous. Handsome. Kind of an asshole. I'll take you a lot of ways, but never easy."

He squeezes back. "I never thought I could have this, you know."

Part of me knows what he means. The love we have together. The sex and the laughter. And more than that, the peace of it. But I want to know which part his heart longed for, so I ask, "Have what?"

"Everything," he says, leaning down for a kiss.

THE END

THANK YOU for reading The Queen! This special print edition contains a bonus scene of the night Penny and Damon met, but unlike the version found in THE KING, this one is told by Damon Scott himself. Turn the page to read it…

BONUS SCENE: DAMON SCOTT

THE LAKE LOOKS almost solid black, the moon painting ripples along the inky surface. Weeds rise up around the edge like teeth rimming a gaping mouth. Mayflies dart above the water, their wings flashing iridescent.

My stomach growls, a physical rumble, and I pull a stick of dry grass from the ground. I've taken to keeping one in my mouth, testing the sharp point against my tongue. It seems to fool my stomach into thinking I'm eating, even if it doesn't fill me up.

Something rustles in the woods behind me. My heart knocks against my ribs in warning. I reach for the knife in my pocket, holding it behind me to hide the glint. The ground whispers against my feet as I crouch.

Leaves dance lightly in the faint wind. Shadows move along the grass.

"Who's there?" My voice echoes back against

the wall of trees.

Nothing. Did I imagine it? It could have been a wild animal. A racoon. A possum. Maybe something bigger, like a coyote. It's probably as hungry as me, but I'm not going to let myself get eaten. As long as it's not a person, I'll be okay.

The snap of a branch.

My eyes narrow. "Come out where I can see you! I have a gun. I'll start shooting if I have to."

One second. Two. Bare feet appear from beneath the brush. Then a pale dress, torn. A dirty face. Wide blue eyes. It's a girl, which doesn't relax me any. "Where's your daddy?"

Her small shoulder lifts. "Dunno."

"You alone?"

"Are you?"

I sense the distrust in her thin voice. That's what finally makes me let go of the knife. "No one comes here. There's nothing but bugs and dirt. And maybe wolves."

Her eyes widen. "For real?"

"Haven't seen one, but I have a knife. I can fight if I have to."

"You don't shoot them?"

Shame rises like acid in my throat. "That was a lie."

That must be the right answer, because she

gives a small nod and steps closer. "Why are you here then? If there's nothing but bugs and dirt?"

"Better than home. Why are you here?"

She doesn't answer, picking her way among the rocks and uneven earth. "You ever go swimming?"

When I need to wash. "Sometimes."

"Are there sharks?"

"Sharks don't live in lakes."

She skirts around me, keeping a good five feet between us. Crouching at the water's edge, she puts two fingers to the surface. Ripples rise around her touch. "What's here then?"

"Alligators, probably."

Her hand snatches back. "You fight those too?"

"Nah, they have to be pretty desperate to go after a person. Mostly they eat fish."

She wipes her hand against her dress, wandering away from the water. Her blue eyes take in my sleeping bag and leftover Styrofoam container from the diner. If I had known she would see that, I would have at least hidden the change of clothes spread out to dry.

My foot nudges the water-logged sex magazine under my backpack.

"You live here," she says, not asking.

Defiance rises up in me, because who is she to judge? "And you live in the trailer park."

Deep in the city buildings lean on other buildings, a large-scale trash pile with only enough space between for people to live. That's where I came from.

Once you get farther out of Tanglewood, you find trailer parks like the one she must live in. I could have stayed in one of the empty trailers, but I could feel the eyes in the park, peeking through broken blinds, watching from beneath frayed curtains. And I don't trust anyone. So I kept going, past the thick brush and trees, the same path she took.

She picks up a stick and draws something in the dirt. A heart.

I stare at the two sides, the way they cross at the bottom, almost awed at her innocence. Definitely horrified. The west side of Tanglewood is no place for a girl as pale and small as her. She's like a white little bunny wandering through a den of snakes.

Of course I might be the worst kind of snake—the desperate kind.

"Go home," I tell her.

"Daddy didn't come back. He went drinking."

"Does he usually do that?"

She nods. "But I ran out of food."

"I don't have any food," I tell her, wishing I hadn't gobbled down the rest of that burger. That was yesterday, but beggars can't be choosers. I only venture into the city once every few days.

She shrugs like she didn't expect anything. "It's okay."

It bothers me that she isn't more angry. Where the fuck is her father? Doesn't he realize what kind of man she could come across, wandering around? "What's your name?"

"Penny. What's yours?"

Would she recognize my name? My father's name. He's notorious in this city. It would scare her, and for some reason I don't understand, I don't want her scared of me.

"Quarter," I say, teasing.

She makes a face. "What do you eat then?"

I glance at the lake. "Fish, sometimes. If I can catch them."

"Like the alligators?"

"Pretty much."

"Did your daddy teach you how to fish?" She makes herself a seat on the flat patch of dirt beside my sleeping bag. It unnerves me how comfortable she seems around me. How comfortable I feel around her. I learned a long time ago not to trust strangers, no matter how pretty or small they may seem.

"No." He taught me other things, like how to steal and lie. How to smile as you strip away someone's humanity. "I don't have a pole or anything."

"Then how do you catch them?"

Reluctance closes my throat. I don't want her to think I'm a freak, which is stupid. She's the girl wandering out of the city with bare feet. "How long can you hold your breath?"

"Dunno."

"Most people can hold it for two minutes. Then carbon dioxide builds up in your blood. Your eyes get dark. And then you take in a breath full of water."

Her eyes are the bluest I've ever seen. "You're talking about drowning."

"I don't drown," I say flatly. "Not for five minutes. Not for ten."

She looks impressed, which makes me feel strangely proud. It's a sick thing to be proud about, considering how I acquired the skill. Being held underwater, for longer and longer.

"Fish don't expect that, a person being so still. And when they're going by me, I stab one with my knife."

Her mouth opens. "For real?"

I shrug, feeling dumb again. It doesn't make sense that I should care what a little girl thinks. She's probably not even ten yet, and I'm almost sixteen. "It's weird."

"I wish I could do that."

"Well, sure. It's on every little girl's to-do list. Learn ballet. See the Eiffel tower. Stab a fish with a knife."

"I wouldn't have to wait for Daddy to come home."

I look at the dark lake, wondering whether I'm willing to go fish for her. Wondering if my backpack will still be here if I do. My small store of cash is inside. "The whole lumberjack outdoorsy trend isn't all it's cracked up to be. There aren't any pillows, for one thing."

"Your Daddy never came back?"

"Oh, he's still there," I say grimly. "That's the problem."

Her small face seems to understand everything. "How long have you been here?"

"Maybe six months." I can't stay out here forever, not unless I want to become a feral animal.

The idea has some appeal, to never return, to

never see another human again. Except for this girl, she's not so bad. I wouldn't mind seeing her again.

"You can stay with me," she says, sounding sure. "I've got a pillow."

The idea sounds ridiculous, but I don't say that. *Her daddy isn't there.* "No."

Her eyes are luminous, almost glowing. "Can I sleep here tonight? I won't get in the way."

For a long moment I study her—her dirty face and her bleeding feet. What a mess. And the way she's holding her breath. She doesn't want to be alone. It's not the hunger that drove her into the woods. It's loneliness.

If I were a good person I would take her back to the city and straight to a police station, let them see how good of a parent her father is. With those angelic eyes someone would help her.

Then again, with that innocent face maybe someone would hurt her. *Shit.*

"Get in the sleeping bag," I say, because I don't have the heart to send her away.

Her small chest rises and falls, faster now. "Why?"

She has enough self-preservation to ask. Men in this part of the city don't care that she's just a kid, not if she's pretty. Or maybe they like that better. I'm not going to mess with her. And I'll cut anyone who tries.

"To sleep," I say with disdain, because that's how she'll trust me. "What would I want with a puny kid?"

And it works, because she climbs gratefully into the plastic fabric, pulling it over her thin legs.

I pull the knife from my pocket. "I'll see if I can catch something, but the fish aren't active at night. And it's harder to see. Pitch black. I have to go by feel."

"Thank you." Her luminous eyes seem almost magical against the dark sky. My chest feels big, like I could take in enough oxygen to last for thirty minutes. Like I could wrestle a whole alligator for her.

Taking a deep breath I submerge myself into the frigid lake.

How many times did my father shove me into a pool of freezing water? Countless. It had been against my will. This time I'm choosing it. The cold shrinks my balls and makes my breath shuddery.

The silt bottom moves between my toes. When I reach the center of the lake I take a deep breath and duck under. It takes three tries, feeling in the ripples for something slippery. When I finally step out of the lake I'm holding a bleeding fish in one hand, my knife in the other.

There's no one curled in my sleeping bag. No blonde hair. No blue eyes.

"Fuck," I say to the empty night, dropping the fish in the dirt.

It gives one last dying flex of its muscles.

My backpack still sits to the side, half-covering the sex magazine. I pull apart the zipper and reach inside. The money is gone. She stole it. I should be mad. I should find her trailer and take it back. Instead I start building a small fire for the fish.

At least she'll have something better to eat.

And please enjoy this scene with Gabriel Miller and Avery James. This occurs chronologically between The King and The Queen. Turn the page to read it.

BONUS SCENE: DAMON SCOTT

THE MOON SITS heavy on the hillside, my constant companion as I build my thesis on the tragic hero. The tragic heroine, to be exact. According to Aristotle, she must make a judgment in error that leads to her own demise. And that makes her weak. It makes her mistaken, but I intend to prove the opposite.

Most nights I'm curled up on the bench that lines a broad bay window, opening to an expanse of land. Like some kind of ancient ruler, I own everything that I see. It's a strangely disturbing sight, one I can't seem to escape, one I wouldn't want to.

In the modern framework of literature, a tragic story is a sad one. But in the context of the early empire, in a society where girls aged twelve were married off to men twice their age, a woman controlling her own fate was a form of power.

Power, even if she died to prove the point.

A shift in the air makes me look up.

There's a faint sound I've come to recognize as the service elevator at the end of the hall. My blood runs faster, thin in the face of old fears. I know I'm safe here, in the expansive penthouse suite that takes up the entire top floor at the Emerald. There's staff and state-of-the-art security that Gabriel had installed when he purchased the entire hotel as a gift for me.

My mind knows I'm safe, even if my body doesn't believe it.

Footsteps down the hallway.

Normally I like how much sound carries from anywhere on the floor. It means I can hear room service coming twenty minutes after I place an order. Or the guard doing his courtesy check with me every evening at turn down. This isn't a big empty castle, haunted and cold. It's full of life.

Except I didn't call for room service.

And I already saw Marco when he came by earlier. He showed me the printout from his wife's ultrasound. Five little fingers on each hand. Pride radiated from him.

Pushing my laptop onto the cushion, I cross the dark room. My phone sits idly on its charger. I glance at the screen. No messages. Should I call Gabriel? The answer comes quickly: definitely not. He would insist on a full sweep of the property, waking up every on-site staff member from their well deserved sleep.

My heart thumps against my ribs, working overtime.

A trauma echo. The words help me refocus on what's happening now.

Not a real threat, even if it feels like that. There's a psychiatrist in the student services office who's worked with me. What Jonathan Scott did to me, what my *father* did to me. They are like the moon looming outside, ever present even though they can't touch me.

The footsteps stop outside the door.

A quiet electronic sound as a key card is inserted—and the door unlocks. An ornate silver handle turns. And a *thud* echoes through the large room as the door fails to open.

I always turn the deadbolt when Marco leaves. And then close the metal latch above the door. And the chain. There are multiple levels of security keeping that door closed.

"Open the door," comes a voice, almost a growl.

The speaker of that voice isn't used to being denied access.

A rush of relief fills the dangerous void in my

heart. I run to the door, heart wild and erratic as I fumble with the locks. Adrenaline makes me clumsy, and it takes three tries to unhook the chain.

I swing the door open, the trauma echo still thundering in my years.

Gabriel stands in front of me, framed by a door he has to duck to enter, his body as immovable as the hills outside my window. "Christ," he mutters. "It's like Fort Knox getting near you."

He doesn't sound annoyed, though. He sounds pleased.

"I thought you were in Nantes until the end of the week," I say, torn between a that soul-deep contentedness I only feel when he's near me and anger that he surprised me.

I don't like surprises, which is why he does them. That's another thing I talk about with the counselor. How grooves are made inside our brains, hardwired pathways where we learn to be afraid or worried.

Gabriel makes his own pathways.

He takes one step forward. I take one back. Another and another, backing me into the room until the wall is flush against my back. Until the door closes with its own weight, leaving us well and truly alone.

In his golden eyes I see something darker—molten arousal. "I couldn't wait."

Every time he breathes in, I feel his broad chest brush against me. And every time I breathe in, I taste his musk and his masculinity. One minute ago I was alone in the stillness. Now I'm in sensual overload, every part of me feeling every part of him, connected by a trust I didn't even know was possible.

"So when you called me this afternoon?" I say, arching my eyebrow.

"I was on a plane."

I try to act stern. "You lied about it."

He doesn't bother saying it was a lie of omission. "Only to please you," he says instead.

And I'm marked by a thousand caresses, by a hundred whispered promises. These are the pathways he makes inside me—pleasure and denial and then pleasure again.

There's a tightness in the muscles around his mouth, a shadow beneath his golden eyes. I run my hand through an unruly lock of his hair, softening at the sight of him.

It's so rare to see him anything but composed. When I had my weekly session with my counselor, when I ate dinner with some friends in the dining hall, when I took the car service back to the hotel. That whole time he must have been on the plane.

"Come to bed," I tell him, knowing he'll take the words sexually.

That's not all I mean—I mean that I want him to find relief in the plush California king bed, that I want him to let down his guard in the way he only does when we're alone together.

It suddenly seems imperative that he takes what he needs from me—from this place, from my body. I want him to find peace, even if it's found with his cock hard and his hands bruising.

Especially if it means that.

I tug his hand toward the bed, but in only one step, two, he's turned the tables.

He's tossing me onto the smooth sheets, landing on top of me, braced on his arms to keep his muscled body from crushing me. His face presses into my neck, and I feel him inhale, goose bumps rising on my skin. He's an animal scenting me, making sure I haven't been marked by another male, a primal instinct that goes beyond words or promises. There's only the pure physical force of him. He drags his teeth along my neck, making me shiver.

"God," I say, my voice thick. How does he do this to me so quickly?

It's overwhelming, having him on top of me, surrounding me. He's all I can see and feel. My whole universe wrapped up in a single rough-hewn man. "You're afraid," he says, his voice hard.

He presses himself between my thighs, his erection thick and pulsing right where I want it most. "Not afraid of you."

"Yes, you are." He places his large palm between my breasts, where my heart beats as fast as it did a few minutes ago, with a stranger's footsteps looming closer. "I can feel you."

I don't want to think about that now. "An echo," I say, trying to pull him close, grasping his muscular arms in a vain attempt to distract him. I might as well move a mountain. "I told you what the counselor said."

He nips my collarbone, a sharp warning for trying to control him. For trying to put a leash on a lion. The pain spreads like warm honey through my body, thick and sweet. "You *are* afraid of me. Not that I'm a stranger coming to your room at night. Afraid that I won't protect you."

There's a hitch in my breath. It gives me away before I can deny the accusation.

It's an arrow to the left of my heart. "It's not you."

"It's you?" he asks, a dark challenge.

"Yes," I plead for him to understand. "It's not that I think you won't protect me. It's that I don't want to need that from you."

He hitches his erection into the V of my sleep shorts, the thin fabric giving away to his heavy flesh, to the precome that's already seeped through his European hand-tailored slacks. "You don't want to need me for anything, do you?"

Only the smallest twitch of his cock makes me moan, a swipe across my clit. "Is that so bad?"

"Bad?" he says, almost incredulous, words thick with fury. "Is it bad that I can't go one minute without wondering about you, wanting you, praying for you? Bad that every breath I take reminds me how far away I am from you, my body in actual pain until I'm close to you again? Bad that I would cut up the damned moon into blocks and build a fort around you if it would help you feel safe? Don't tell me this isn't bad, little virgin. It's a fucking tragedy."

The word blooms inside me, both familiar and new again.

A tragedy, that this man should be on his knees and made helpless by arousal. That he should need me as much as I need him. A tragedy that he loves me.

"My tragic hero," I whisper. "My own."

I don't know whether the error in judgment was mine or his. All I know is that we're both powerful in this, both made stronger by the heat that courses between us. I lean back on the bed, pulling him close not with the force of my arms but with the steady regard of my gaze.

When he flips me onto my stomach, it feels right. The way he his hands roughly yank down my sleep shorts, only far enough that he has access to me, the fabric keeping my thighs pressed together.

Then he thrusts inside me, hard enough to make me whimper.

It only makes him move faster, harder, one hand at the back of my neck, the other holding my hips steady. It's a cruel and dominating possession. It's a tender mercy fuck. We are both at the same time, moving in tandem, fighting each other even as we work towards the same goal.

His cock slides over the swollen walls of my sex, making me clench tight on every thrust. The orgasm winds through me like smoke above a fire, curling its own design through the darkness. I come in a flash of white, my body clamping hard on his, drawing a tortured groan from his lips, pulling the climax from his powerful body.

We collapse onto the bed together, both of us made soft by passion, made strong by promise.

In the modern framework of literature, a tragic story is a sad one. But in the context of a dark underworld, in a society where young virgin women are auctioned off to wealthy criminals, a woman controlling her own fate is a form of power.

Power, even if she fell in love to prove the point.

Thank You

Thank you so much for reading THE QUEEN! I hope you absolutely loved Damon and Penny's story. This was a book close to my heart. It was an honor to write it.

If you haven't yet read Gabriel and Avery's books, start with THE PAWN. And if you have read the Endgame trilogy, find out what happens between Harper and her step-brother Christopher in SURVIVAL OF THE RICHEST. *Two billionaires determined to claim her. And a war fought on the most dangerous battlefield—the heart.*

And don't miss Anders's book, THE BISHOP!
  A million dollar chess piece goes missing hours before the auction.
  Anders Sorenson will do anything to get it back. His family name and fortune rests on finding two inches of medieval ivory. Instead he finds an injured woman with terrible secrets.
  He isn't letting her go until she helps him find the piece. But there's more at stake in this

strategic game of lust and danger. When she confesses everything, he might lose more than his future. He might lose his heart.

Turn the page for an excerpt from OVER-TURE...

EXCERPT FROM OVERTURE

*R*EST, LIAM TOLD me.

He's right about a lot of things. Maybe he's right about this. I climb onto the cool pink sheets, hoping that a nap will suddenly make me content with this quiet little life.

Even though I know it won't.

Besides, I'm too wired to actually sleep. The white lace coverlet is both delicate and comfy. It's actually what I would have picked out for myself, except I didn't pick it out. I've been incapable of picking anything, of choosing anything, of deciding anything as part of some deep-seated fear that I'll be abandoned.

The coverlet, like everything else in my life, simply appeared.

And the person responsible for its appearance? Liam North.

I climb under the blanket and stare at the ceiling. My body feels overly warm, but it still feels good to be tucked into the blankets. The blankets *he* picked out for me.

It's really so wrong to think of him in a sexual way. He's my guardian, literally. Legally. And he has never done anything to make me think he sees *me* in a sexual way.

This is it. This is the answer.

I don't need to go skinny dipping in the lake down the hill. Thinking about Liam North in a sexual way is my fast car. My parachute out of a plane.

My eyes squeeze shut.

That's all it takes to see Liam's stern expression, those fathomless green eyes and the glint of dark blond whiskers that are always there by late afternoon. And then there's the way he touched me. My forehead, sure, but it's more than he's done before. That broad palm on my sensitive skin.

My thighs press together. They want something between them, and I give them a pillow. Even the way I masturbate is small and timid, never making a sound, barely moving at all, but I can't change it now. I can't moan or throw back my head even for the sake of rebellion.

But I can push my hips against the pillow, rocking my whole body as I imagine Liam doing more than touching my forehead. He would trail his hand down my cheek, my neck, my shoulder.

Repressed. I'm so repressed it's hard to imagine more than that.

I make myself do it, make myself trail my hand down between my breasts, where it's warm and velvety soft, where I imagine Liam would know exactly how to touch me.

You're so beautiful, he would say. *Your breasts are perfect.*

Because Imaginary Liam wouldn't care about big breasts. He would like them small and soft with pale nipples. That would be the absolute perfect pair of breasts for him.

And he would probably do something obscene and rude. Like lick them.

My hips press against the pillow, almost pushing it down to the mattress, rocking and rocking. There's not anything sexy or graceful about what I'm doing. It's pure instinct. Pure need.

The beginning of a climax wraps itself around me. Claws sink into my skin. There's almost certain death, and I'm fighting, fighting, fighting for it with the pillow clenched hard.

"Oh fuck."

The words come soft enough someone else might not hear them. They're more exhalation of breath, the consonants a faint break in the sound.

I have excellent hearing. Ridiculous, crazy good hearing that had me tuning instruments before I could ride a bike.

My eyes snap open, and there's Liam, standing there, frozen. Those green eyes locked on mine. His body clenched tight only three feet away from me. He doesn't come closer, but he doesn't leave.

Orgasm breaks me apart, and I cry out in surprise and denial and relief. "*Liam.*"

It goes on and on, the terrible pleasure of it. The wrenching embarrassment of coming while looking into the eyes of the man who raised me for the past six years.

Want to read more? OVERTURE is available on Amazon, iBooks, Barnes & Noble, Kobo, and other book retailers!

MORE BOOKS BY SKYE WARREN

Trust Fund Duet

Survival of the Richest

The Evolution of Man

North Security series

Overture

Concerto

Sonata

Underground series

Rough

Hard

Fierce

Wild

Dirty

Secret

Sweet

Deep

Stripped series

Tough Love
Love the Way You Lie
Better When It Hurts
Even Better
Pretty When You Cry
Caught for Christmas
Hold You Against Me
To the Ends of the Earth

Standalone Books
Wanderlust
On the Way Home
Beauty and the Beast
Anti Hero
Escort

ABOUT THE AUTHOR

Skye Warren is the New York Times bestselling author of contemporary romance such as the Chicago Underground and Stripped series. Her books have been featured in Jezebel, Buzzfeed, USA Today Happily Ever After, Glamour, and Elle Magazine. She makes her home in Texas with her loving family, two sweet dogs, and one evil cat.

Sign up for Skye's newsletter:
www.skyewarren.com/newsletter

Like Skye Warren on Facebook:
facebook.com/skyewarren

Join Skye Warren's Dark Room reader group:
skyewarren.com/darkroom

Follow Skye Warren on Instagram:
instagram.com/skyewarrenbooks

Visit Skye's website for her current booklist:
www.skyewarren.com/books

Copyright

This is a work of fiction. Any resemblance to actual persons, living or dead, business establishments, events or locales is entirely coincidental. All rights reserved. Except for use in a review, the reproduction or use of this work in any part is forbidden without the express written permission of the author.

The Queen © 2017 by Skye Warren
Print Edition

Formatting by BB eBooks

Made in the USA
Columbia, SC
26 June 2023

19407374R00171